FRANCO
&
GRUBBER

and the Pearls of Nebulus

FRANCO
&
GRUBBER

and the Pearls of Nebulus

Kerri Anderson

Boarstone Publishing

First published in the UK by Boarstone Publishing
www.boarstonepublishing.com

ISBN: 978-0-9933222-0-4

Cover introduction: Howie Firth
Editing: Sarah Eddie
Proofreading: Jade Moores

Typeset in Plantin Light by Palimpsest Book Production Ltd
Falkirk, Stirlingshire

Printed by TJ International Ltd
Padstow, Cornwall

To Maarten

Chapter One

A metallic bug, shaped not unlike a kidney bean, was drifting purposefully through the depths of outer space, its chromium shell glinting in the afterglow of a dead planet. No lights bleeped on its dashboard, but it seemed to know where it was going.

Meanwhile, aboard the craft, a fight was taking place in the rear, although to describe it as a fight would give the impression of two beings facing each other, fisty cuffs up and ready to make violent contact.

Instead a giant stalblagger was holding a human at arm's length in the air by his neck, and trying to decide what to do next. 'I will have you,' it burbled. 'I will have you tell me why you are here.'

Franco, for that was the human's name, had no intention of telling anyone anything, and was pretending to look like a dead chicken, mainly because he was finding it hard to breathe at this point and so imitating a hippo would have been ridiculous.

'You will not pretend to be a dead chicken,' the stalblagger burbled. 'I will pass you through the Ring of Truth, and you will speak.'

'That's just an old tyre someone's left burning on the floor,' squeaked Franco.

'Do not decry the Ring of Truth.' The creature's voice was rising. It had been ready to have a snooze, and now the snooze would be cold.

'But how can you pass me through it if it's lying on the floor?' asked Franco, before returning to his dead chicken routine.

The stalblagger paused, deep thoughts passing over its head. 'I had not thought of that. Hmmm. If I put you down, will you promise not to run away, and will you help me raise it up?'

'Sure,' said Franco. 'Have you got any rope?'

The creature rummaged around in its belly. 'No, but I have a spare eyeball on a length of elastic. Will that do?'

'Great!'

'Now what do we do?'

'If you hold up the tyre, and I'll swing the elastic over that beam up there and then tie it through the middle of the tyre, and Bob's your uncle.'

'I do not know any Bob.'

'Yes, but I'm sure he'd love to meet you.'

'Do you think so?'

'Absolutely. After all, Bob is your uncle.'

The stalblagger grew misty eyed. 'Uncle Bob is the best. I love my uncle.'

'What about this tyre?' asked Franco.

'I am missing my uncle, and you want to talk of tyres?

How can you be so cruel?' It wiped its nose on its arm, and then stuck it back in place.

'Sorry,' said Franco. 'It's just that earlier you seemed so keen, you know, to stick me through the Ring of Truth and all that, and now it's like your heart's not in it anymore.'

The stalblagger's eyes were welling up. 'I have been so lonely on this mission, and Uncle Bob was the only one who really knew me.'

'I'm sure he'd be really proud of you, out on this mission of yours. What is your mission by the way?'

'To seize all the broogle mines in the solar system and crush the people with a mighty fist.'

'If you don't mind me saying, your craft seems to be rather on the small side, no offence, especially if you're wanting to carry broogle.'

'We have backup.'

'Okay.'

'So,' sniffed the creature, 'you really think my uncle would be proud of me?'

'Absolutely, I mean, all that people bashing and broogle seizing, what's not to be proud of?'

The stalblagger visibly perked up. 'Why are you being so nice to me?'

'Well, it's not every day you get to do a dead chicken impression.'

But now the creature was standing up straight and looking purposeful. 'Right, enough of this chit chat, where were we?

Do not decry the Ring of Truth. I will pass you through it and you will speak.'

'We've done that bit,' said Franco.

'Have we?'

'Yes, look at the script.'

'Oh, so we have. Where are we then?'

'You were going to hold up the tyre, and I was going to tie it to the beam.'

'Okay.'

'Ready now. On the count of three, pick up the tyre, and remember to bend your knees. Oh, you don't have any. Well, on the count of three, and remember to bend. Three.'

'Huh?'

'You're meant to pick up the tyre,' Franco whispered.

'Sorry,' whispered the creature. 'Do you think they noticed?'

'No, they're too busy reading. Okay, we'll try again. Ready this time?'

'Ready.'

'Three.'

The stalblagger grabbed the tyre with all available hands, and then dropped it. 'Aaaaah, aaaaah! My hands. My hands are burnt. My hands are burnt. Aaaaah! Uncle Bob, help me.'

'Here he comes!' yelled Franco.

The creature turned to look. Grabbing his chance, Franco ran in the opposite direction, opened the nearest door, and disappeared behind it.

It was a cupboard. Realising that there wasn't room for

4

him and all the used sweetie wrappers inside it, he backed out, only to find a stalblagger with singed hands bearing down on him.

'Nephew!' cried Franco, throwing out his arms. 'Got a hug for your Uncle Bob?'

The stalblagger stopped in its tracks and squinted at him. 'Uncle Bob? Uncle Bob? If you are Uncle Bob, then why do you look like the prisoner I was interrogating?'

'You mean there's a guy going around impersonating me? Why, that's shameful. Let me at him and I'll make sure he doesn't pull that stunt again.'

'And he did this.' The creature held out its burnt hands.

'Shocking. We can't allow this sort of behaviour to go on. Where is the scoundrel so I can show him what's what?'

'He's in that cupboard there.' The stalblagger pointed.

'What? This one?'

It nodded.

'Okay, stand back. Let me deal with this.' Franco banged the door. 'Now listen here, whoever you are. You can't go round burning folk's hands and expecting to get away with it, you, you. . .'

'Scoundrel,' whispered the creature.

'Thanks. You scoundrel. And as for impersonating a. . . a. . . what the hell was it?'

'Uncle Bob.'

'What is it?' asked Franco.

'For impersonating an Uncle Bob.'

'What? Yes, of course.' Franco raised his voice. 'For impersonating an Uncle Bob. That deserves, that deserves. . .'

'Eyebrow pickling,' squealed the creature.

Franco turned. 'Eyebrow pickling?'

It nodded vigorously.

'Okay, your call.' He turned back. 'That only deserves eyebrow pickling, my friend.'

'He's not your friend,' whispered the creature.

'Yes, but he doesn't know that,' whispered Franco.

'Oh. Right. Yes, yes, not your friend.' The stalblagger pulled the eyeball on elastic back out from its belly and gave it an excited ping.

'Please, this is serious,' said Franco.

'Sorry,' said the creature, and popped its eye back in.

'Okay, this is where things get nasty,' said Franco, taking the creature by the arm and leading it towards the rubbish disembarkation chute. 'I don't want you getting hurt, so best if you hide in here while I deal with it.'

'But Uncle Bob.'

'No buts.'

'But Uncle Bob, what about the eyebrow pickling?'

'Once I'm done, he's all yours.'

'Oooo goodie.' The creature gave an excited shiver.

'Now fold your arms in tight, close your eyes, and I'll pull this lever here.' There was a whooshing sound, followed by a burp, and the stalblagger disappeared down the perspex tube.

'So long sucker,' said Franco. 'Now, time to get this lump of metal out of here.' He went to the front of the craft and eased himself into the pilot's seat, bringing it down from stalblagger height, then back up again when he realised he couldn't see out of the windscreen. 'Okay, let's see how this baby rolls. Lights, lights, lights, where are the bloody lights? No, that's not it. Nope, nope.'

A huge beam of light filled the cabin, illuminating the whole ship.

'Not quite what I was after. A bit too visible, but it'll have to do for now. Important thing is to get moving.'

'Do not move,' boomed a disembodied voice. 'There is no point. We will only catch you and crush you if you do. Therefore, opposition is futile, unless of course you like being crushed, ha, ha, ha. Meanwhile, please enjoy some light snacks and music while we prepare for your internment.' The voice clicked off and was replaced by a bland twinkling of notes, while a bowl of select crinkle cut crisps appeared at the side window.

'Might as well,' said Franco, and let the bowl in.

A few minutes later, the music came to an abrupt halt.

'Please vacate your seat and step out of your craft, bringing with you any dirty crockery so that we may wash it and use it again,' intoned a pre-recorded female voice. 'We hope you have enjoyed being held captive by us and that you will consider being held captive by us again, in the unlikely chance that you escape.'

'You want me to step outside my craft? Are you nuts? That's straight into outer space, so it is,' said Franco, still eating the last of the crisps.

'That's what I said,' said the voice, and turned off the lights.

'Hey, I thought you were pre-recorded,' said Franco.

'I am. Now move it.'

7

Franco stood up, just as the lights went out. 'Ooyah,' he yelped, forgetting the height of the chair as he tried to clamber down and cracking his knee off a control panel. 'That's really helpful, that is. If you're wanting to get me out of here, the least you can do is give me some light to do it by.'

There was a second's pause, and a glow light came on in the cabin.

'Gee, that makes all the difference. Now at least I'll be able to see what I've walked into after I've walked into it,' he grumbled.

The glow light grew momentarily stronger, enabling Franco to find the exit and stumble out into what should have been outer space. Instead he was grabbed on either side by unseen hands and placed on an escalator, which carried him up and then through a pair of curtains, depositing him on a small platform near the back of a vast hall.

'How's my hair?' asked a grey lump of a creature, sitting on a large throne-like chair in the midst of the hall, to an aide standing nearby. 'Are the lights catching my profile at its most sublime?'

'Indeed sir, they are,' said the aide.

'And the script? Where's my script? How am I meant to be word perfect for my performance?' He gave a harrumph and cleared his throat, coughing up onto a sheet of paper as it was handed to him. 'Get me another copy. What do you mean that was the only one? Get me last time's script then. Do I have to do all the thinking round here? It's not like he's ever heard it before, is it?'

'He's here, sir.'

'Who's here?'

'The prisoner, sir.'

The golgor captain squinted across to where Franco was standing. 'Well, tell him to get behind the curtain. I'm not ready yet. Go on, get back behind the curtain, you.' He flapped the paper at Franco. 'And where's my script? Someone appears to have coughed up on this one.'

It wasn't so easy trying to get back behind the curtain, Franco found, when the escalator insisted on pushing him onto the platform.

'What on earth is he doing?' asked the captain, reading glasses perched on the end of his nose and new script in hand.

'He's trying to go back behind the curtain, sir,' said the aide.

'Why's he trying to do that?'

'You asked him to, sir.'

'Did I? Well, I'm ready now, so you can tell him to stop that. You there, stop that. What's happened to my spotlight?'

'Sorry,' called a voice.

'Why am I always destined to work with amateurs? No matter, the speech must be made.' He gave a little cough. 'Across the aeons of ages, through the mists of time and back again, the Crest of the Helms of Golgor is the might of the stars, the power that shall seize, making all bow before it. This is good, isn't it?' he said, turning to an aide. 'In fact, I almost wrote it myself, you know. Where was I?

9

Ah yes, making all bow before it. For only then shall the Golgors. . .'

'Sir.'

'At the rightful zenith of destiny that was. . .'

'Sir.'

'What is it? I'm just hitting my stride. This had better be good, subtenant.'

'It's nearly tea and biscuit time, sir.'

'Why didn't you say so? Okay, how much time have I got?'

'About thirty seconds, sir.'

'Is that all? Hmm.' He ran his finger down the page. 'Master of all, blah, blah, blah, tremble before, blah, blah, blah, shall now deny, blah, blah, infringement of airspace and subsequent capture on suspicion of proprietorial acquisition ameliorated through long-term excavational incarceration. There, that should do it.' He took off his glasses and looked up. 'How was I? You can be honest. I was dreadful, wasn't I?'

Franco realised the captain was addressing him. 'Oh, um, em,' he stumbled, not sure what the captain was getting at.

'The speech, man, the speech. How was I?'

'Um, very concise.'

'Concise? Concise you say? What else?'

'Decorative without being flashy.'

'It's tea break time, sir.'

'Never mind that now, subtenant. Take a note of what the prisoner is saying. I want a copy sent to General Huffenpuff. Then we'll see who the loquacious old windbag is. My performance,' said the captain, turning back to Franco. 'What about my performance?'

'Your performance was. . .' Franco searched for the right words, 'Um, stately and um. . .'

'And what, man, and what?'

'. . . insightful.'

'Insightful, you say? In what way?'

'Captain.'

'Not now subtenant. In what way insightful?'

'Reflecting a greater knowledge and understanding than would be otherwise expected.'

The captain's eyebrows twitched. 'Are you trying to say I look thick?'

'Oh no, what I meant was. . .'

'Sir, screen two.'

'Not now. Explain.'

'Than would be otherwise expected in a military. . .'

'Because if you think I'm thick, you should. . .'

'Sir.'

'Just put a snowball aside for me. I'll eat it in a minute.'

'Sir, screen two,' said an aide

'Screen two, screen two, what's all this screen two? Can't you see I'm in the middle of. . . ah, General! Didn't see you there.'

One of the screens on the far wall crackled into life, and a small image appeared in the middle of it.

'In fact, I still can't see you.'

'Damn,' squeaked a voice. The screen crackled again, and the view of a gargantuan golgor who would have been deemed somewhat on the unattractive side on a good day loomed into view. 'Better?' asked the deepened squeak.

'Doubtful,' muttered the captain. He raised his voice. 'General Huffenpuff, you're looking well.'

'Enough slithering Captain. We both know I'd frighten the jelly out of a bowl. Now have you got your song sheet ready?'

'But I was about to go for tea and biscuits.'

'Looks more like you were in the middle of boring the pants off some prisoner. What is it? Some kind of narkle?'

'He was found on a stalblagger scout craft heading towards the Sector Quadrant.'

'Does he speak?'

'Indeed he does. He was telling me how insightful and stately he found my speech.'

'So, not very bright then.' The general snorted. 'You, narkle, can you sing?'

Franco stared.

'Speak up. Can or can't you?'

'I used to be in my school's choir.'

'Is that a yes?'

Franco nodded.

'Pass him a song sheet then. I'm sure you can't be any worse than the good captain here.'

An aide handed some lyrics to Franco, while another wheeled out a piano and then began banging out a rather oompah oompah rhythm on it.

'Ah, *The Heave Ho Song*, if I'm not mistaken,' said the general. 'Song sheets high, people, and no wobbly Bs. All together now.'

12

'Heave ho me boys,' bellowed the general.

'We're off to see the space rocket,' trilled the captain.

'Heave ho me boys,' echoed Franco.

'It's such a sight to see,' chimed the aides.

'With laser beams and speedster streams

And twiddily bits that go aaah!

It's a bit of a pain to watch a plane

Go into the back of a car.'

'Ha, ha! Great stuff. I love those twiddly bits.' The general wiggled his fingers in demonstration, causing the captain to roll his eyes. 'Anything wrong Captain?'

'No sir. Just looking for the next song.'

'Well, I doubt you'll find it on the ceiling. What's next then? *My Spacecraft's the One on Top*? *The Rubber Duck Waltz*? I know, *Don't Float Your Dinner in Space, Dear.*'

'May I suggest *Cosmos the Comatose Comet*? It has a terrific chorus,' said the captain. He drew in a deep breath, ready to sing, at which point the aide began beating out the same oompah oompah rhythm.

'Suggest away Captain, but it looks like we're doing *The Five and Three Song.* You'll like this one, narkle. A real crowd pleaser.'

'What do you do when you've got five aliens?

What do you do when you've got just three?

What do you do when you've got five aliens?

Send them down the mines and then have a cup of tea.

'What do you do when you've got five laser beams?
What do you do when you've got just three?
What do you do when you've got five laser beams?
Cut up a banana and then sit it on your knee.

'What do you do when you've got five spacerships?
What do you do when you've got just three?
What do you do when you've got five spacerships?
Grab another ten and take o'er the galaxy.'

'Well, I don't know about the rest of you, but that's really set me up for the rest of the day. "And take o'er the galaxy." Terrific stuff. Captain, a pleasure as always, although careful with that vibrato. We don't want to have to replace the piano again. And you, narkle, shame you can't be with us next time, but such is life. Grand Fall to you all then, and a high salute.'

'Grand Fall,' chorused everyone except Franco, as the general fizzled off screen.

'And an effin' high salute,' muttered the captain.

'I heard that,' squeaked a fading voice.

The captain turned around red faced and glared at the room. Clearly his day had been set up differently to that of the general's. 'Enough dallying around,' he snapped. 'Thanks to our dear general, we will have to reschedule tea break and bring forward the afternoon performance. But what can you do when you're forced to work with rank amateurs and buffoons. Subtenant, prepare my eye gel pack. I feel a headache coming on.'

14

'What about me?' Franco was still standing on the platform, his song sheet having been taken off him.

The captain, about to head out the door, stopped and looked at him. 'I thought I made it perfectly clear earlier: long term excavational incarceration. It's down the broogle mines with you. See how far your singing voice gets you there.' And then he went.

'Don't worry. It could be worse,' said an aide, taking Franco by the elbow and guiding him down a long corridor.

'Could it?'

'No, not really,' admitted the aide. 'I'm just trying to cheer you up. But look at it this way, at least you don't have to sing with the captain again.'

'Every cloud.'

'I'm sorry?'

'Nothing. So, how long am I down this mine thingy for?'

'Until your teeth fall out or you go mad. Whatever happens first.'

'Huh?'

'If it's any comfort, if your teeth fall out you usually go mad soon afterwards anyway.'

'Gee, hold me back. Anything else I should watch out for while I'm down there?'

'Don't be tempted to eat any of the broogle. It only makes your teeth fall out faster.'

'A bit devil and the deep blue really, isn't it?'

'Sorry?'

'Nothing.'

'Well, here we are. This will be your holding pen until we

reach the mine you're going to. Lucky for you we haven't picked up too many others this round. Oh look, someone's waving at you. That's nice, someone to chat to.'

Franco peered in. It was a waving stalblagger.

'In you go then. It's been nice meeting you, and good luck in the mines. Remember what I said about eating the broogle.'

'I'll remember,' said Franco, and tapped his teeth.

Chapter Two

'Everybody out,' called the bulk monster. 'Those of you with four arms or more, please follow my associate here who will issue you with your regulation pickaxes. The rest of you, follow me.'

Franco rubbed the cramp out of his ear. It had only taken five hours to explain that just because he looked like Uncle Bob didn't mean he was Uncle Bob; that he was in fact Uncle Bob's identical twin brother, a kind of two for the price of one offer, and because he was the two and not the one that meant that they weren't technically related.

'You two together?' The bulk monster stopped suddenly and turned to face them.

'He is my Uncle Bob,' said the stalblagger, patting Franco on the head.

''Course he is. Come with me, I've got just the job for the pair of you. Rest of you, wait here. You two, this way.' He led them up a small tunnel that ran off the main part of the broogle mine, and unlocked a door. Inside was shelf upon shelf of underpants. 'We need these bagged up for collection. Clean ones in the laundry bags. Dirty ones in

17

the incineration bags. You'll find tongs over there. Good luck gentlemen.' And with that, he locked the door behind them.

Franco cautiously picked up a pair of underpants and gave them a long-armed sniff. 'Guess there's only one thing for it. We'll use your eyeball and elastic to fire the underpants at that wall there. Any that are dirty will stick to it, and we can peel them off with the tongs. The clean ones'll fall down, and we can line the laundry bags along underneath to catch them. Simple.'

The stalblagger looked doubtful.

'Think of it like a game of squash, but with added aroma,' said Franco.

The creature clutched its eye.

'C'mon. Do it for your Uncle Bob. Then I'll show you how we're going to get out of this place.'

'But why do we want to get out of this place?'

'Because we've got to leave before our teeth or our senses do, that's why. Look, let's at least give it one go, and if your eye doesn't like it, you get it straight back. This does mean we'll have to examine the pants more closely, but if that makes you happy then that's how we'll do it.'

The eye was cautiously handed over. 'Will this burn my hands?'

'Is that what's bothering you?'

The stalblagger nodded.

'Only if we put you in one of the incineration bags by mistake. Now, hook the elastic through a leg hole and tie it round. Right, stand back a bit and hurl!'

18

The underpants shot across the room, smacked into the wall, and then fell into a crumpled heap.

'Better get those laundry bags lined up underneath the wall there. See, you give it a go.' The stalblagger picked up a different pair of pants, threaded the eye through them and *Wap!* they spread themselves against the wall and stayed there. The stalblagger giggled.

'A well-worn pair there methinks. Grab the tongs and pop them in an incineration bag. That's it. Okay, want another go?'

The creature nodded. *Whizz!* Another pair shot across the room. *Wap!* It slid down the wall. *Whee!* The next pair stayed there. The two of them took turns; while one was busy underpants whizzing, the other would rush around picking off the ones that had stuck to the wall and putting them in a bag. Soon they were both giggling as pants, stripy, spotty, creased, holey and plain filled the air, so much so that neither noticed the elastic on the eyeball was getting thin until it all of a sudden burst, sending the eye smacking off a lurid orange pair.

'My eye!' shrieked the stalblagger and ran to console it.

'Is it okay?' asked Franco, genuinely worried at the thought of now having to examine the pants by hand. He looked at the frayed elastic in his hand. 'Hold on, I know!' He grabbed a pair of extra generous underpants, tore a hole in the waistband, and whipped out a nice long length of nearly new elastic.

'Look, Blagger, look. See what I've got.' He dangled the elastic at the creature. The stalblagger looked up from

19

stroking its eye, snatched the elastic off Franco, and turned to face the wall. There was a small pinging sound, then a bigger one, and a bigger one, until suddenly the eye shot across the room, narrowly missing Franco's head, and landed back in the stalblagger's hand with an almighty whack. The creature grinned.

'You nearly had my eye out there,' snapped Franco. The stalblagger merely continued grinning and gave the eyeball a suggestive dangle, before popping it away in a skin fold.

'Like that is it then?' said Franco. 'Well, I wouldn't like to be the one who has to individually sniff each pair of pants 'cause they wouldn't share their eyeball with another person, even though it was that other person who managed to repair it, so I wouldn't. Incidentally, where have those tongs gone?'

The stalblagger, appearing to pay no attention to Franco's little rant, continued scrabbling around in its skin and, finding something that appeared vaguely edible, proceeded to chew it after a cursory inspection before realising it was in fact a spare light bulb and sticking it back where it found it.

'Ah, gentlemen. Hard at work I see.' The door had swung open and the clipboard-wielding bulk monster was once again tapping it officiously. 'Not many bags done, eh? I'd leave you to finish the job, but there's a blast of broogle needing cleared on Level Four, and we're a bit short staffed, so it looks like you gentlemen are needed there. This way please.'

'What about the escape plan?' whispered the stalblagger

to Franco as it skipped along behind the bulk monster in an awkward attempt to keep up.

'Funny, I thought you might have tried to escape in one of the laundry bags. That's what they usually do, until they find out the whole lot gets incinerated anyway,' said the bulk monster, striding ahead.

'That was it,' whispered Franco.

'That was what?' whispered the stalblagger.

'That was the escape plan.'

'To turn us into laundry bags?'

'Not exactly.'

'No whispering, gentlemen. Did no-one tell you it's rude to whisper?'

'Sorry,' they chorused, jogging behind.

'Watch out for those teeth there. They're a bit slippy.'

'So it's true about making your teeth fall out?' asked Franco.

The bulk monster stopped and leered down into Franco's face. 'How else do you think I got these babies?'

Franco gulped. 'Very nice,' he said, as the sight of yellow teeth glinting in a mouth of blackened gums appeared before him.

'Now, unless you'd like to fill the vacancy for a back molar, I suggest you gentlemen shut up and the sooner we get to Level Four, the better.'

But before the bulk monster could stand up straight again, the stalblagger wheeched out the tongs, grabbed the monster's nose and twisted him round so he was now bent over backwards and grimacing upside down. Franco stared at the stalblagger in surprise, who winked, and then pressed the tongs shut even harder.

'Ma nose, ma nose! A canna breath!' The monster's arms began flailing.

'Listen here, pal,' said Franco, taking advantage of the situation. 'Either you tell us a way to get out of this place that doesn't involve incineration or pants,' he grabbed one of the monster's front teeth and gave it a little wiggle, 'or you'll be setting up an account with the tooth fairy.' Franco withdrew his hand, and the tooth came with it. 'Oops, didn't mean to do that there. Sorry.' He stuck it back in its rotten hole, where it sat wobbily. 'See, good as new.'

'I'll get oo for 'at,' said the monster, and keeled over.

'Think you might have been pinching a bit hard there,' said Franco, as they looked down at his massive fallen form.

'Sorry,' said the stalblagger.

'No worries. I don't think he'd have told us the way out anyway. Now, let's see if he's got anything on him that will show us a way out of here.'

Their searching revealed the clipboard, which turned out to be blank, a jar of peppermints and a tub of earwax.

'Go on then,' said Franco, who could see the stalblagger eyeing up the earwax.

It grabbed the tub, and tucked it away with the tongs and the eyeball.

'We may as well bring these too,' said Franco, picking up the clipboard and peppermints. 'At least then we won't arrive at the party empty handed.'

'What party? I know of no party.'

'Neither do I, but you never know. Now let's get moving before another one of these cretins decides to put us on broogle duty.'

And lo, it was that they soon discovered the magical power of the clipboard. If anyone stopped to question why two prisoners were wandering around the mines, especially when they passed the same way half a dozen times, the tapping of said clipboard soon put a stop to any awkward questions, and they were back on their way, and then back again.

'Bloody hell,' said Franco, 'this place can't be that big. I mean, if there's a way in, there's a way out, even if it's the way in.'

'Oh no,' said the stalblagger. 'The mines are famous for their complex structure and inescapability.'

'And how do you know all this, Brainbox? Oh, I forgot, your lot were planning to take them over and crush them with a mighty hand.'

'No, I read it in the leaflet.'

'What leaflet?'

'This one.' The stalblagger held it up.

'Give me that here.' Franco snatched it. 'What kind of mine has leaflets?'

'It also has a gift shop. Look.' The stalblagger pointed it out excitedly.

'And everyone knows gift shops are always on the way out. Come on.'

'But how will we find it?'

'By trying to avoid it. There's no avoiding a gift shop. Okay, which way Snappy?'

'Who is Snappy?'

'You are. You know, ping, ping, ping, snappity snap snap, eyeball on elastic.'

The stalblagger stared doubtfully.

'Well, if Snappy doesn't float your boat, how about Snappers or Snapdragon. No, a bit girly. I know, how about Snap? Anyway, pick a direction. We can argue about the finer points of what to call you later.'

'But why must I pick?'

'Because you want to get to the gift shop, and I don't. So, if you pick the direction we'll never find it because you never find the shop when you're looking for it, then we take the opposite direction, which guarantees we will find it. Whereas if I pick the direction, and I don't want to go to the shop, then I'm guaranteed to pick the right – or is it wrong? – direction and therefore, just pick one, will you? Left or right?'

'Left.' There was the faint sound of elastic pinging. 'Uncle Snappy.'

A greasy pompom-like creature prepared to scuttle past, but thought better of it on sight of the clipboard. They watched it go.

'Right it is.'

'I do not understand why you should want to avoid a gift shop. Surely it is a place of wondrous things, of shimmering lights and captivating baubles.'

'And overpriced pencils. Which way now, Snap?'

Silence.

'Which way now?'

'Right.'

'Left then.'

They followed a long corridor through the depths of the mines, with no passages leading left or right off from it, until they eventually came to two identical doors sitting side by side.

'Think carefully now. Which one should we open?'

The stalblagger swithered. 'Um, ah, um.'

'Think of all those snow globes with real teeth floating inside, the "You don't have to be mad to work here but you will be soon" t-shirts, the "Wish I wasn't here" postcards, the spiral bound notepads with photos of pigs on the front that no-one remembers ordering but are somehow always there. Think of them all, think.'

'Um.'

'You're almost shaking that snow globe, aren't you?'

'Yes.'

'You can feel it in your hands.'

'Yes.'

'Now choose.'

A momentary pause, then the stalblagger's arm shot out and pointed. 'That one.'

'Looks like we're going in this door then. Hope you packed your wallet for the snow globe extravaganza.'

The stalblagger crossed its fingers and closed its eyes in anticipation.

'And in we, oh.'

For a gift shop, it was doing a good impression of a sauna.

'Hurry up and shut the door. You're letting in a draught,' said an indistinct pink blob through the steam.

'Sorry,' said Franco and the stalblagger.

'Well, sit down then.'

They sat.

'Now, what are your two fellow's names?'

'I'm, er, Sidney, and this is Rudolph.'

'I'm Grandling, and over there you've got Bladog and Swillig.'

Vague outlines waved through the steam. Franco and the stalblagger waved vaguely back.

'Sidney? Is that a Subterranean name?'

'Um, no.'

'Pity, I've got a sister there. Lovely sauna though, eh?'

'Eh, yes, lovely,' said Franco. 'Actually, we're looking for the gift shop.'

'Can't help you there. Bladog, Swillig, ring any bells?'

There were murblings of dissent.

'Sorry, fellows. What do you want one of those for, especially when you can sit here in this lovely sauna?'

'Rudolph here collects snow globes.'

'Ah, I see your problem. Have you tried next door?' The pink blob beamed at this excellent idea. 'I'm sure they could help. I'd show you the way, but I need another ten minutes in here, or is it fifteen? Anyway, just next door. I'm sure you'll find it.'

'Thanks. Come on Rudolph, let's get moving.'

'My skin's shrunk. I cannot move,' said the stalblagger.

'Terrific. Now what?'

'Problem there, Sidney?' asked Grandling.

'Yes, my friend appears to have shrunk his skin and can't get up.'

'Hold on a sec. I know just the thing.'

There was an almighty thwacking sound, a cry of pain, and the stalblagger shot up and out of the door.

'The old whack 'em on the bottom with a towel trick. Never fails. Remember to close the door on your way out now.'

'Guess you didn't want that snow globe hard enough,' grumbled Franco, as a still shrunken stalblagger struggled on behind. 'Well, this door had better be it. Ah, this looks better.'

Dusty boxes were lying around the floor, and the shelving had long given up trying to display anything with any kind of decorum. And there were no snow globes.

'Guess that leaflet of yours is a bit out of date.'

'Rudolph' said nothing, but only partly because its facial skin was still on the tight side, and pocketed a couple of Yvonne rubbers and a Garry felt tip pen.

'Doesn't look like there've been any tours through here for a while,' said Franco. He shuffled his hand through a pile of postcards and pocket calculators, then, 'Ah! Fudge! I could go a sugar buzz.' He burst open a box and stuck a handful in his mouth. As he chewed, he took a closer look at the box. '"Fludge. An exotic blend of finest dairy and extravienne effluent." What! I'm chewing butter and shite. Bleuuuu!' He spat it out. 'Although,' he grabbed another couple of pieces, 'it isn't half bad', and stuck them in his mouth.

A few thoughtful chews later Franco said, 'Time to look for the exit.' He turned to look for 'Rudolph'. 'What's up with you Reindeer Boy?'

The stalblagger was standing staring at a shiny red coin operated spacecraft ride with a large propeller on the front and a big yellow peep peep horn. Admittedly it was somewhat on the small side, but that couldn't stop 'Rudolph' salivating at the sight of it.

'Come on, we haven't got time for this,' said Franco.

'But I've always wanted to go on one. It has been my dream.'

'Well, do you have any change on you?'

The stalblagger shook its head sadly.

Franco glanced around, spotted what he was looking for, and stuck a couple of them in the slot.

'Hopefully they won't start melting before the machine realises they're chocolate coins and not the real thing. Well, go on then, hop on.'

The stalblagger looked briefly at the craft, which had already begun moving, and scrambled in. It grabbed the steering wheel and a look of fierce concentration spread across its face. 'Uncle Bob, Uncle Bob, you too, you too.'

'No, not really my style.'

'Please, pleeeeeeease.'

'Oh, alright then.'

'Rudolph' beamed. Franco squeezed in alongside it, and the two of them sat there being jiggled to the strains of

Hector the Happy Spaceman as the little craft motored on its rotating plinth, with the occasional toot toot from the horn.

All too soon it was over.

'Thank God,' said Franco, and leapt out.

'I want to go again,' said 'Rudolph', and burst into tears.

'No more. Remember, we're only here to find a way out.'

'But you have more coins.'

'Not now I don't,' said Franco, and ate them.

'I hate you,' said the stalblagger.

'Fine. See if I care. Actually, what do I care? If you want to spend all day on a toy ship and risk getting caught, feel free, but I'm getting out of this place. Now, where have they hidden the exit?'

But it was too late for finding anything except somewhere to hide, as a couple of bulk monsters, very similar to the first one, but minus the charm, barged into the shop and knocked their way through the cardboard boxes. Franco spied the clipboard lying out of reach on top of the pocket calculators, and, realising he was left defenceless, dived behind an ill-fitting display of bouncy mushrooms. 'Rudolph' remained where it was.

The pair didn't seem to notice anything amiss, lost deep in a professional grumble about someone in the higher echelons.

'And I said, do I look like some effin' flying bicycle or what?'

'What did he say?'

The first bulk monster gave his ear a small tug. 'Doesn't

really matter. Point is, you can't let the sluggards get away with it. You've got to let them know what's what.'

'You still going to the work's picnic?'

'Nope.'

'What about the Broogle Bash?'

'Nope.'

'Or the Upwelly Helly?'

'Same.'

'He didn't like the bit about the bicycle then?'

'You could say that. Now, are we going to get that ice-cream maker or what? I want to get out of here. Gift shops always give me the creeps.'

The two of them began rolling a battered-looking metal box towards the door.

''Course, if it was up to me,' said the first bulk monster, 'I'd pack in this whole broogle nonsense and get a proper job like winkle-lifting or, or. . .'

'Or,' said the second one, 'how about. . .'

They both began laughing.

Trying to get a view to see what was apparently so funny, Franco leant just a little too far forward and sent a whole shower of bouncy mushrooms cascading down from the shelves in front of him.

'Did you hear something?' asked the first bulk monster.

'No,' replied the second.

'Me neither. Hey, what's up with your face?'

The second bulk monster was now looking decidedly pale.

The first monster turned to see what he was looking at.

30

'Aaaaargh!' he screamed. 'Mushrooms, mushrooms! Run for your life.'

They dashed for the exit, the mushrooms bouncing after them in hot pursuit, and slammed the door shut behind them.

'See, I told you gift shops were creepy,' said the first bulk monster.

'It's safe to come out now,' called Franco, once the mushrooms had calmed down and there was no sign of the monsters coming back. 'That was a close one, Slackskin, eh? Thought they were going to make ice-cream of us for a moment there. Wonder what flavour we'd turn out to be? A mixture of earwax, chocolate coins and fludge, mmm-mmm. Yes sir, give me two cones of your finest waxochoc fludge sludge ice-cream there, and no scrimping on the earwax shavings.'

The stalblagger had nodded off in the little spaceship and appeared to have slept through the whole event.

Franco gave it a vicious poke with a sparkly straw.

'Yo, Slacky, you been listening to a word I've been saying?'

'I must return the porcupine to the land of the womble,' mumbled the stalblagger.

Franco gave another poke.

The stalblagger shot up from its slumped position and gazed uncomprehendingly at the strange little man gesticulating wildly with a shiny stick from in amongst a sea of giant mushrooms. It decided that the world it had just come from made far more sense and shut its eyes in a determined

31

attempt to get back there. And it might have worked if the little man hadn't insisted on poking it again, only this time with a biro.

The stalblagger stared.

'Come on, what are you staring at? I've just saved your bacon from getting fried by those couple of monsters there. Not that you were any use 'cause you were too busy sleeping.' Franco was getting annoyed.

What was this talk of bacon? the creature wondered. It gave a quick rummage through the contents of its skin. No bacon. The bacon was gone.

'This is no time for a scratch. We've got to get going before those guys get an urge for vanilla and stalblagger crush.' Franco started wading through the mushrooms, sending them bouncing across the floor, but without their earlier enthusiasm.

'I have no bacon. Where have you saved it? Give me my bacon back,' the stalblagger roared.

'What are you talking about? I haven't got any bacon.' Franco was searching in a storage cupboard. 'No, nothing here.'

'But you said you saved my bacon.'

'Yep, and you think you'd be a little more grateful about it.'

'Give me my bacon back.'

'I haven't got any bacon, you daft twonk. Now get off that machine and get looking for the exit.'

'I want my bacon.' The stalblagger grabbed Franco round the neck and held him aloft. 'Give me back my bacon.'

Not this again, thought Franco. 'It's a figure of speech,' he squeaked. '"Saving bacon." Like "how's your father", or "'til the cows come home."'

'My father is a cow?'

'Well, that's not for me to say. Look, let me down. We haven't got time to do the whole chicken and ring routine.'

Franco's fall was broken by one of the mushrooms.

Thoughts were flickering round the stalblagger's eyes. 'My father is not a home-coming cow?'

'Precisely,' Franco puffed.

'And I have no saving bacon.'

'Correct.'

At this the stalblagger sat down and started to cry.

'Don't worry.' Franco patted him on the arm. 'I'm sure your father never wanted to be a cow in the. . .'

'But I want my bacon,' wailed the stalblagger.

Franco glanced around nervously. 'Can you try wailing a bit quieter? Somebody might hear you.'

'But my bacon.'

'There is no bacon. Look, how about the next time your bacon needs saved I chuck in a couple of onions and leave you to get on with it? How does that sound?'

The creature gave a sniff and nodded.

'Okay then, better now?'

It nodded.

'All ready to find the exit now?'

Another nod.

'And, just to check, do you remember who I am now?'

'Uncle Bob,' it whispered.

'I can't hear you.'

'Uncle Bob.'

'And again. C'mon, give it power.'

'Uncle Bob,' yelled the stalblagger quietly, and punched the air.

'Yeah!' Franco punched the air too. Then something caught his eye. 'Of course! God, why didn't I notice it before? The turnstile. Over there.'

And there it was, lurking under a pile of commemorative tea towels.

The stalblagger gave a sniff and looked over. 'But there is no door on the other side of it.'

'That's what they want you to think,' grinned Franco. 'Cunning fellows, those designers, keeping you here until every last scented candle is gone. C'mon, let's go for it.' Franco tossed the tea towels aside, turned the bar and pushed through. 'Your turn,' he called from the other side of the unseen door.

Only hesitating to grab a last ruler, the stalblagger squashed its large frame past the unyielding metal, and the gift shop disappeared.

Chapter Three

Clouds. Fluffy white clouds. Lots of them, floating above the ground like headless sheep, while above the sky shone a brilliant cloudless blue.

'God, some exit that turned out to be,' grumbled Franco. 'My trainers are getting soaked. Nobody ever tells you you need wellies in space. It's stupid having clouds on the ground anyway.' The stalblagger ignored him and continued skipping as only a stalblagger can, which is badly. 'They're probably not proper clouds anyway. Probably some post-industrial speuch from the mining process. In fact, I probably shouldn't even be breathing this stuff.' He gave an exploratory cough. 'Probably. Hey, are you listening to me?'

But the stalblagger was off, bouncing over a particularly fluffy cloud, and about to disappear behind an even fluffier one.

'Yo, Skippy,' called Franco. 'Don't go dancing too far ahead now. We might have made it past the turnstile, but we're not out of here yet. And those bulk monsters might come out looking for us. I wouldn't fancy your chances with Mr Clipboard, not after that stunt you pulled with the tongs.

Are you listening? Hey, what the. . .' He turned to see what kind of cloud could be hard enough to bump into him and found himself face to bonnet with the rumbling engine of a minibus.

'You fellas need a lift?' A cheery-cheeked apple-faced man stuck his head out the driver's window. 'He is a guy, your pal, isn't he? Only you can't tell with some of them.' He gave a sniff.

'Yo, Cynthia! Start dancing this way. We've got a lift,' yelled Franco and threw a last chocolate coin at the stalblagger. 'Cynthia', not too pleased at this apparent chocolate subterfuge, began kicking its way back through the clouds, coin in hand, and an expression on its face like the back end of a turfburger.

'You know, for a female, she's got a right good left hook on her,' said Franco. The driver paled and pulled his head back in through the window.

'Hurry up,' yelled Franco again, then mumbled, 'Before Pippin here changes his mind.'

'So, where are you boys headed?' Once it had been explained that for stalblaggers, Cynthia was a name of honour and meant 'He Who Hammers Nails in With Head', everything was fine, although the driver still blinked a few times every time the name was said.

'Em, we're off to a party,' said Franco.

'You are?' said the bus driver.

'We are?' asked 'Cynthia'.

'Where about?' asked the bus driver.

'I'm not sure. We haven't been invited yet.'

'Haven't we?' The stalblagger was confused.

'No.'

'Why not?'

'They don't know we're coming.'

'Why not?'

'I haven't told them.'

'Why not?'

'Long story.'

The stalblagger gave Franco a hard stare.

'Really long story,' said Franco.

The bus driver started chuckling. 'A right pair, you are. Don't know if you're coming or going, or if you should have come when you got there.' His chair bobbed up and down in unison with the chuckling.

'So,' said Franco, changing the subject, 'how come you were driving past?'

'I still drive past now and then. Still get the odd one or two visitors stumbling out, so I always like to drive past, 'cause you never know, you never know.'

'When d'you last pick up someone?'

The driver sucked his teeth. 'Oooo, must be, what, getting on for ten years ago now. Right fellas, where d'you want to go? 'Cause as you can see, we're just about to run out of road.'

They leant over to look out of the window, and, sure enough, the road was about to come to a sudden end, along with the ground.

'Is he trying to kill us?' whispered the stalblagger.

'I think so,' said Franco.

'Final chance to state your destination, guys.'

'Aaaaaaargh!' screamed Franco and 'Cynthia' in unison.

'Funny,' said the driver, 'that's where the last lot asked to go too.'

Chapter Four

'That was a bit of an overreaction, don't you think?' grumbled Franco, giving a rainbow a swift kick when the stalblagger wasn't looking.

(It turned out the creature was rather partial to rainbows and kept sticking them in its pockets. Later it would be mystified to discover them full of water instead.)

'I mean, I only threatened to strangle him for pretending to take us off the road. Not my fault he's got a sense of humour like the back end of a squirrel.' Franco and the stalblagger were once again kicking around in a land of white fluffy clouds, the driver having deposited them right back where he'd found them, and they were finding it as much of a scintillating experience as before.

'And see these bloody mints we found? They're bloody hard. In fact, ooyah, I think I've cracked a filling. Come and have a look.' Franco opened his mouth wide, taking care not to swallow the offending mint.

The stalblagger, who could apparently hear him after all, despite signs to the contrary, skipped over, and steadied itself to perform a cursory check (humans were famous for their noxious breath, and so it didn't want to take any chances). Suddenly, its eyes goggled and even the spare eyeball started pinging around on its elastic.

'What? What's the matter? Spit it out.'

The stalblagger said nothing, reached again for the tongs, and removed the sweet.

'Bleuch! Bleuch! Yuck! God, you're disgusting. Those tongs have been in who knows how many unidentified aliens' underpants, not to mention up a bulk monster's nose, and you're sticking them in my gob. Are you some kind of psycho or what? What the. . .'

He fell silent, as they both looked upon the mint, glowing softly as it sat between the arms of the tongs.

'What the. . .'

'The Pearls of Nebulus,' whispered the stalblagger in awe. It raised the tongs higher, and the pseudo mint responded by glowing momentarily brighter.

'What the. . .'

'Tales are told of the Great Oysters of the Minty Mouthwash, where each one produces a pure pearl once every hundred aeons, a pearl so pure and luminous that anyone who beholds it is overcome by its beauty and radiance.'

'Do you often talk like a travel brochure?' is what Franco might have said if he'd been less overcome with emotion. Instead what he said was, 'That thing nearly bloody broke my tooth. In fact,' he probed around his mouth with a finger, 'I wouldn't be surprised if it's cracked a back molar.'

'Those who become a vessel of a pearl,' continued the stalblagger, 'temporarily take on some of its properties, and those around them cannot touch them. "A vessel you will know by their radiance and glow."' It scanned Franco up and down, and sighed.

'What's up with your face, Grandad? Anyone'd think it was you who'd nearly lost a tooth. God's sake.' Franco stopped whining to aim a kick at a particularly persistent cloud, when the cloud decided to back off and evaporate. 'Ha! Serves it right. Bloody cl. . .'

'Your feet,' whispered the stalblagger.

'My feet? What you going on about my feet for when it's my mouth you should be worrying about?'

It pointed with the tongs, and the pseudo mint pulsed in recognition.

Franco looked. His trainers were sparkling white, almost glowing, and Franco himself was hovering above the ground, barely, but enough.

'The tales say that the power of the pearl can be found in the purest part of the vessel.'

'In my feet?'

'In the purest part.'

'But I can't have washed them for days.' He paused. 'The purest part you say?'

There was a moment's silence.

'Do you have any more?' asked the stalblagger.

'Only the other ones that were in with it.' Franco produced the jar of peppermints he'd taken from the bulk monster. '*Pearls of Nebulus*' read the label.

'Well, blow me,' said Franco. 'I thought they looked a bit funny.'

41

The stalblagger carefully screwed off the lid and dropped the still glowing, although less so than before, pearl in beside the others. Then it wrapped the jar in a pair of clean underpants, and tucked it away under a fold of skin.

'What did you say they were called?'

'The Pearls of Nebulus.'

'And they have special powers?'

'Indeed.'

'Which make the purest part of you light up?'

'It is so.' The stalblagger nodded solemnly.

'So.' Franco started to grin. 'Let's see which part of you lights up if you suck one.'

'Stalblaggers may utilise the Power of the Pearl, but we are not overcome by it.'

'Bollocks. I bet your eyeballs start to glow or your skin, or, or your skin goes all see through and I can get to see just what kind of clobber you've got hidden under there.'

'It is not so.'

'Ah, bullshit. I bet it does, and you don't want me finding out, which is why you've now hidden the jar. And what's with all the Yogic donkey talk all of a sudden? Just earlier you were begging me to let you have another go on a toy spaceship and now you're acting like you're the Sage of the Gates or something.'

'The Guardian of the Third Eye.'

'You what?'

'Mastix is the Sage of the Great Gates. I am the Guardian of the Third Eye.'

'Yeah, and I'm King of the Bollocksphere.'

'There is no such thing.'

'That was kind of my point. Likewise your claim as. . .'

'We destroyed it.'

'Destroyed what?'

'The Bollocksphere. We destroyed the sphere with a mighty fist.'

'Now where have I heard that before? Look, I've no idea what you're on about with your Third Eye bollocks and Pearls of Nebulus. My point is this. . .'

The stalblagger waited.

So did Franco.

'Um, who's Mastix?'

'My cousin.'

'Right.' Franco looked thoughtful. 'And see when they made your cousin Sage of the Day.'

'The Sage of the Great Gates,' corrected the stalblagger.

'Quite. Did they give them a shitty little space craft and a burning tyre, sorry, I meant, a highly sophisticated inter-stellar transporter and the Ring of Truth, and kick them into space, I mean, send them on an important scouting mission?'

If it is possible for stalblaggers to sneer, that is what this one did. 'No,' it sneered. 'Mastix is merely the guard of the gates of our beloved planet whose vast lands are a sight to. . .'

'Cut the infomercial. Did they give Mastix anything else?'

'A very large key.'

'For the gate?'

It nodded.

'Anything else?'

The stalblagger thought. 'Merely the password.' Then blinked. 'But not an important mission such as mine. For where I go, others follow, and there will be a mighty fist that will. . .'

'Did they give you the password?' Franco interrupted.

It blinked again.

'Let me run a scenario past you here. They make you, now let me get this right, they make you Guardian of the Third Eye, give you a mission, a spaceship and a burning ring.'

The stalblagger beamed.

'I'm on the right track so far then, am I? Then they stick you on said craft, wave you through the gates, and it's at this point they make Mastix, was it?'

It nodded.

'They make Mastix Guardian of the Great Gates, give them a whacking great key and the password, upon which, I'm not going too fast for you am I? Just say if I am.'

The stalblagger shook its head.

'Upon which point, your cousin wields the key, locks the gate, and you're on the other side without the password.'

The stalblagger blinked. Again.

'Am I right?'

The stalblagger continued to blink.

'That, my friend,' said Franco, 'is what is known in the trade as a right royal stitch up, class A1. Get rid of your clapped-out craft by getting some bozo to fly it off for you.

Even better, convince them they're on some kind of fancy mission, and it's sayonara, shit ship, so long boz-oh!'

Tears were now leaking from the stalblagger's eyes, despite the rapid blinking, and its nose was in danger of losing its facial grip.

'Oh, slap me sideways and call me a banana. You didn't think I meant any of that, did you, did you? I say all sorts of bizarre things when my blood sugar's low. Remember, all I've had's some fludge, and, well, we know what was in that, and a mint that wasn't even a mint at all. Look, here, blow your nose on this.' He handed the stalblagger one of its own arms and gave a good rub. 'See, that's better, isn't it?'

The stalblagger nodded.

'Not so bad after all, eh? You shouldn't go round listening to everything I say. I can be a right narkle sometimes, especially when my belly's rumbly.'

'Narkle,' sniffled the stalblagger.

'Yeah, a right narkle.'

'Numpty narkle.' It gave a little giggle.

'Numpty narkle, that's me,' said Franco, puffing up his cheeks and moving from side to side like a fat chimpanzee.

'Numpty narkle with a fizzwig for a nozzle.'

'Okay, no need to get personal,' said Franco, less chimp-like now.

'Numpty narkle with a fizzwig for a nozzle and a slumpity slump slump.' The stalblagger's sides jigged with laughter and tears sprang anew, but from a different source.

'Okay, okay.' Least I wasn't daft enough to get myself locked off a planet without the password to get back in.'

All laughter ceased, and the pair stared grimly at each other.

'Well, I wasn't,' said Franco, hands on hips.

The stalblagger wished it'd left Franco down the drain where it had found him, even if it had rendered the toilet unusable. But it never said this, only made the sound of a U-bend being unblocked, followed by the sound of running water.

'Like that, is it?' asked Franco.

The stalblagger pulled itself up to its full height and reached for a loo brush.

'Two can play at that game,' said Franco, and rifled through his pockets. Seconds later he was brandishing a vicious looking bus ticket and a pair of nail clippers.

Thus armed, they squared up and prepared for combat, Franco demonstrating the clipper action, the stalblagger flicking the loo brush bristles ominously.

There was a polite but audible cough.

Franco and the stalblagger eyeballed each other, not an easy thing when one of you is five foot four and the other has heights of grandeur.

The cough was followed by a gentle tap on Franco's shoulder.

Franco looked around, then down.

'You dropped this,' said a small pompom-like creature with knobbly arms, holding up the bus ticket.

'Not now. We're kind of busy,' said Franco, as a loo brush came crashing down on his head.

'Perhaps you would like it,' said the pompom, turning to the stalblagger.

Never one to turn down the offer of acquiring something, the stalblagger bent over to take a closer look, and promptly felt the sharp end of the nail clippers in its backside.

'I would keep it,' continued the pompom, 'except it's out of date, and they don't run buses on this route anymore. But I can deposit it in the nearest waste receptacle, should you so wish, although strictly speaking it is your responsibility.'

This was all lost on the pair, who were unable to hear due to bruised egos, and wounds the size of their imaginations.

The pompom tutted, put the ticket in a pocket somewhere, and walked off.

'Hoy!' yelled Franco, temporarily coming out of his loo brush concussion. 'What was that about a bus?'

The pompom walked on, accompanied by the sound of jangling.

'Hey!' Scrambling to his feet, Franco stuck away the clippers and began running after the creature, closely followed by the stalblagger and its brush.

'What was that you said about a bus?'

Although they'd caught up, the pompom continued walking, the jangling sound coming from a bunch of keys in its hand.

'If you'd listened to me in the first instance,' said the pompom, 'you would have distinctly heard me say that there are no longer any buses on this route. However, I do have a car, and should you be requiring of a lift, I will be willing to oblige. I would request though that you refrain from dropping litter, and that you keep your feet off the uphol-stery. Also, that any beverages you have upon you must be consumed before entering said vehicle.' At this the pompom stopped and looked at them with fixed blue eyes.

'Anything you say, pal,' said Franco.

'Quite,' said the pompom.

'Where is it?'

'Here,' said the pompom, and opened the door of a bright red mini.

'So,' said Franco, leaning forward from the back passenger seat, 'where are we headed?'

'Please sit back in your seat and refrain from moving around. It impedes my view of the rear mirror,' said the pompom, adjusting the mirror with a leather driving gloved hand.

'Shouldn't you do that while you're still stationary?' Franco pointed out.

The pompom said nothing, but Franco could have sworn that the car heating had been turned down.

The stalblagger also said nothing, on account of being strapped to the car roof and unable to hear the conversation inside. It instead amused itself with little ditties of what it was going to do to Franco and the superannuated snowball once it was unstrapped.

The pompom flicked the windscreen wipers on briefly, then off again, then fiddled with the radio. Heavy rock music came booming out of the speakers, the pompom tapping gently along with one finger on the steering wheel. After the singer had let out a final blood curdling shriek, the radio was snapped off, and silence resumed.

'So,' said Franco, cleaning the blood out of his ears, 'you like music then?'

The creature did not reply, but removed the lid from a tin of mints, popped one in its mouth, and replaced the lid.

'Oh ho,' said Franco, in the manner of one waiting to be offered, and pointed. 'Hope you checked the label on those first.' He gave a who-me?-are-you-sure?-well-okay-then-I'll-take-two chortle.

The pompom's face frowned slightly in the mirror.

'You know, one of those mints that isn't really a mint; it just kind of makes you glow instead.'

The pompom's face changed to mild panic. It picked up the tin, glanced at the back. 'Sugar free,' it confirmed and put the tin down again.

Franco sighed, and sat back in his seat. He then spent five seconds examining his nails, ten seconds gazing out the window at the passing clouds, sighed loudly, checked his nails again, and leant back forward.

'So.' The word hung there while Franco tried to think of a follow up that didn't involve asking for a mint.

'This is where you get out,' said the creature, speaking first, then bringing the car to a halt.

'It is?' All Franco could see was the same cloud filled landscape they'd started with. 'Are you sure? I mean. . .'

'Quite.'

'Couldn't you. . .'

But the pompom was already up and out, and untying

the stalblagger. It quickly checked for damage, stepped back in the car, and sped off. Seconds later, the sound of heavy rock music could be heard fading into the distance.

Once more, Franco and the stalblagger found themselves marooned in the middle of a cloud drenched landscape, but this time without a turnstile to keep them company.

'Well,' said Franco, grasping the enormity of the situation, not liking it, and, so, letting it go again. 'How rude was that? Not that I wanted a mint anyway. Still, it's the principle, don't you agree?'

And the stalblagger may indeed have done so, if it wasn't already flagging down the very same red mini, somehow coming from its original direction.

The mini stopped, and a white fuzzy head popped out of the driver's window. 'You fellas looking for a lift?'

'Is this your idea of a joke? C'mon Snappy. We don't need being messed around. If you don't mind, we're off to get our own mints. Snappy?'

'Snappy' was already squashed into the back seat.

'Hurry up,' said the pompom, 'we don't want to be late for the Buffet.'

'Food?' Franco was in the car like a shot.

There being no room in the back, even with the stalblagger's head out of the sunroof, Franco was forced to sit in the front, next to a tin of wine gums.

'Help yourself,' said the pompom with a wave of a gloved hand.

'Well, if you're sure.'

'Here.' The pompom held out the tin to the stalblagger, who took it, tipped out the sweets, and handed them back. The pompom chuckled, and tossed the sweets into its mouth.

'Hey. What about? Where's my. . . ?'

'Never mind,' said the pompom, patting Franco's knee. 'You can have the tin next time. But no time for all that now. Goggles on and off we go.'

Four pairs of goggles swung down. Suspicious of putting them on, Franco turned to see what the stalblagger was doing. It already had two pairs on, and gave Franco a jolly little wave.

'This buffet had better be good,' he muttered, and pulled on his goggles, just before the mini suddenly increased in speed, pinning them all back in their seats and pushing their eyes to the back of their heads.

It was hard to judge how long they'd been speeding forward, but when they finally did slow down, Franco knew it would take more than a sausage roll and a couple of twiglets to get rid of the sore head he now had. He was temporarily distracted from the pain by the site of 'Snappy' in the rear view mirror practising shadow puppets. That, and the sight ahead of an enormous phalanx of red minis arranged in a huge circle, the other side of which disappeared over the horizon.

'Ah, I see Vincent has kept us a space,' said the pompom, pushing up its goggles, and puttling the car into a gap in the circle.

And even though one white fluffy pompom wearing driving gloves looked very like another glove enhanced pompom, Franco was sure he'd seen this one before. The same recognition had obviously passed through the stalblagger's head, as it was once more holding the loo brush.

'Ah Vincent, good chap,' said the second pompom. Vincent scowled briefly, and then the two pompoms headed off together into the ring of cars. And, since they weren't sure what else to do, and since, presumably, where the pompoms went, the Buffet would be, Franco and the stalblagger followed.

'God, this buffet had better be good. I'm starving,' said Franco to his companion-in-situ. 'Although I'm beginning to wonder if these guys aren't one loop short of the full pompom, if you know what I mean.'

The stalblagger gave the air a swipe with the brush.

'Hey, you're nearly hitting me with that thing. Put it away. And I hope you cleant it before you nicked it. You did, didn't you?'

The stalblagger said nothing, just quietly tucked the brush away.

'God, you're disgusting, you are. I bet they won't let you near the sausage rolls when they find out what you're carrying. What's that look supposed to mean?'

The stalblagger gave Franco a sideways glance, and then hung an air freshener off his nose.

'Ha, ha. Very funny.' Franco wiped it off with his hand. 'Just make sure you use a napkin to pick anything up. I'm still feeling a bit dodgy after that fludge. Ah, looks like we're here. God, would you look at the size of that queue.'

Where once there had only been two pompoms, there

were now a whole array making their way forward. It was enough to make anyone sneeze.

Franco sneezed. The array quickly became a horde that got denser and denser, ever moving forward, until Franco and the stalblagger looked as if they were wading through an extreme deep-pile carpet. The ground began rising until they couldn't see what was beyond the top of it, only the sight of pompoms disappearing over the edge.

'Great. We're surrounded by suicidal dust bunnies. I opt we head back now and borrow one of those minis. It's not as if they'll be needing them the now.'

But there was no option. The crowd kept moving them forward, until they reached the edge.

And discovered themselves entering a huge natural amphitheatre. Its scale was enormous, and every patch of it was covered in pompoms. The sight was surprisingly unnerving, like realising you've just spilt ink on a new carpet, and that no amount of scrubbing will make it better. It will only make it bigger.

In the very centre was a bare area of ground. Franco could just make out a desk, and possibly a pompom sitting at it. It was hard to be sure, dazzled as he was by the sea of white fluff.

As if thinking the same thing, the stalblagger handed Franco and itself a pair of sunglasses.

The crowd had stopped pushing forward and appeared to be settling where it was. Then the possible pompom stood up, at least that's what it looked like it was doing, it was hard to tell through such dark sunglasses.

'These sunglasses are really dark,' said Franco.

'Grand Bacon,' called the possible pompom.

'Grand Bacon,' called back the crowd.

'My bacon,' said the stalblagger.

'Yeah, and not much room on that table either for a buffet, not with this size of crowd,' muttered Franco.

The crowd sat en masse.

Franco and the stalblagger sat too.

'Maybe they're bringing the plates round. Probably the only way they can get rid of the fish paste sandwiches. I hate fish paste sandwiches. The only time I ever ate one was. . .'

The stalblagger elbowed him to shut up.

'Welcome to the Buffet,' cried the pompom.

The crowd murmured in reply.

'About bloody time,' muttered Franco, before the stalblagger stuck a dummy in his mouth.

'You all know why we are here today.'

The crowd sat in silence.

'The situation is becoming intolerable,' continued the pompom, its voice sharp and clear. 'Our demands have not been met. For too long we have been taken for granted. For too long we have been sidelined, ignored, forgotten, set aside. We have been pushed too far.'

The crowd shuffled in agreement. Somewhere someone unwrapped a crinkly sweetie. A Mexican wave of disapproval shimmied round the amphitheatre.

The possible pompom gave a short cough, then began again. 'For too long we have had late returns. For too long

54

we have had notes in the margin. For too long we have had biscuit crumbs and jam between the pages.

'Today, my fellow librarians, is where it stops. No more overdue books, no more unpaid fines, no more cutting the coupons out of the communal newspaper. Silence shall once more mean silence, and the consumption of food and drink shall once more be punishable by death, that, or a severe ticking off, depending on local jurisdiction or departmental policy. Please refer to your departmental head for clarification in this area.

'From this day forward a return date will mean exactly that: the date by which a book must be returned. Death, fire or disease are no excuse for crossing this line anymore.

'Fellow librarians, I call on you to use the tools at your disposal: the Disapproving Frown, the Tut of Disgust, the Cold Shoulder, and the Condescending Tone. Only then can we begin to reclaim our rightful status, to reclaim the respect that is due to us as Guardians of the Folios of Knowledge. If that means fewer visitors across our threshold, so be it. If that means removing all day sleepers from the reference section, let it be so. And if that means being shut on unexpected days of the week to allow for staff training or because of little-advertised local holidays, it will be done.'

Applause fluttered briefly in the air, then stopped as softly as it had started.

'As Chief Librarian, I realise the onerous task I put on each of your shoulders. It will not be easy. You will have to be ever vigilant for cookery books deliberately misfiled under Regency Romance, and for the misappropriation of pens for home use. But if this task was easy, it would mean that *anyone* could be a Librarian.'

The air grew momentarily cooler, as a lifetime's worth of pompoms collectively sucked air in through their teeth in an expression of disgust at this very thought.

The Chief Librarian paused. 'Now, let's dance.'

Music suddenly came blasting out of unseen speakers. If the sight of en masse pompoms was enough to rattle your roots, imagine those same pompoms wigging out to *I Will Survive the Apocalypse Now*. Unsure whether to join in or not, Franco and the stalblagger sat there impassively as little skinny arms flailed around them and fluffy white bodies bobbed up and down for all they were worth.

Then it was over. All the dancing abruptly ceased. Each pompom bent down, picked up a goody bag that definitely wasn't there earlier, took out the false nose and glasses inside, put them on, and walked off whistling.

Too stunned to move, the duo continued sitting there until the whistling had stopped and the place was empty. They slowly reached down, and, sure enough, there was a little carrier bag for each of them too. A root around in it revealed the same false nose and glasses (which they duly put on over their sunglasses), a tin of sweets, a key fob ('Hey, I never got one of those,' said Franco), a pencil, and a notepad, all emblazoned with the phrase 'National Librarian Donkey Sanctuary'. Although, strangely, the pencil also had printed on it 'This Way Up'.

Franco held it 'This Way Up', but nothing happened. So he stuck a sweetie in his mouth instead and sulked about the key fob. 'So, what do we do now?' he asked, once the sulk was over and he realised he would probably never have used the fob anyway and it would just have gathered dust in the bottom of a drawer somewhere, but, still, it would have been nice to at least have had the option.

The stalblagger shrugged, then ate the key fob.

They sat there munching. The sound echoed around, but since there was no-one there to shush them, it wasn't a problem. No-one, except an old man in a brown overall, pushing a broom.

The man came over, the broom arriving before him.

'Good Buffet?'

'I've had better,' said Franco, and popped in another sweetie.

'Only, if you don't mind me saying,' said the old man, 'you don't exactly look like librarians.'

'We're trainees. Part of a new initiative. Broaden the scope beyond the more traditional areas of recruitment,' said Franco. The stalblagger nodded in agreement.

The old man smiled. 'Very good, very good. Only, if I may be so bold, you're not exactly the right shape for going up and down access tubes, are you?'

'Say what?' Franco peered at him over the top of the false nose and glasses. 'Why on earth would we be doing that?'

'Oh dear, oh dear,' said the old man. 'Maybe you haven't reached that stage in your training. I hope I haven't spoilt things for you. Only, they closed down all the libraries years ago. Nowhere for the librarians to go. The only work they could get was as dusters, cleaning out ventilation systems and the like, you see. That's why I was surprised at your, um, shapes. Not very shaft friendly, if you don't mind me saying. Still, maybe they're introducing a new shaft system. Like you said, broaden the scope.'

'So what was all that stuff about returning overdue books and jam in the creases?'

The old man shook his head. 'So sad, so sad. The loss of status was more than they could handle. They could not admit their change in circumstances to themselves or to each other, so each year they still hold their annual conference as if nothing has happened. And a very nice time they seem to have too. Ah well, must be pushing on. There's a group of engineers coming in later, and we all know what they can be like!' He waggled his eyebrows. 'Best of luck with your training.' The broom started moving, and where it went, the old man followed.

'Wonder what's in their goody bag,' said Franco. 'Maybe they do decent food. God, I'm starving.'

'There's a burger van on your way out,' called the old man, who, by now, was nearly halfway round the amphitheatre. 'Tell them I sent you.'

Chapter Five

'Two burgers, no, better make that four, one banana milk-shake, one chocolate. Definitely chocolate? You're sure now? Not raspberry?' asked Franco.

'Chocolate,' said the stalblagger.

'One chocolate milkshake, two packets of ready salted and a packet of bacon crisps. Oh, and a couple of chocolate bars, in case we get peckish later.'

'Is that all?' asked the creature behind the counter.

'Yup.'

'That's fifteen chocolate coins then.'

'How much?'

The creature, who looked like the van had been built around him, put his hands down on the counter. 'Fifteen chocolate coins.'

'But the prices on the board mean it should only come to five.'

'You said the old man sent you, didn't you?'

'Yeah.'

'Well, that makes it fifteen. Old bastard keeps forgetting

59

his wallet. Keeps saying he'll send someone round with the money. All right?'

'Guess so,' said Franco, not wanting to argue. 'Fifteen, you say?'

'Yup.'

'Right.' Franco shuffled in his pockets with the slow realisation that chocolate coins might be one thing he didn't have on him. And the smell of those burgers was fair making his tummy rumble. 'Um, Sparky, old pal, give the gentleman the chocolate coins. I'll square with you later.'

The stalblagger duly began rummaging through its skin, pulling out all sorts of junk, but no money. 'It must be in my other skin,' it whispered to Franco.

'Your other skin? You mean, you have more than one?'

It nodded.

'You're kind of gross, you know. Other skin.'

The creature began tapping on the counter.

'Um, it looks like we've encountered a slight problem here,' said Franco. 'It looks like my friend here has neglected to pack its wallet. Perhaps there's something else we can offer you in exchange.'

'No money, no food.'

'Oh, um.'

The stalblagger nudged him and handed Franco the jar containing the Pearls of Nebulus. Franco gave it an are-you-sure? look. The stalblagger nodded.

'Perhaps though you would make an exception with this,' said Franco, holding out the jar.

'It's a jar of mints,' said the creature in the van.

60

'That's what it may look like to the casual observer. In fact, we made that same mistake ourselves. But these "mints", as you call them, actually have special powers. You just have a wee sook on one, and all sorts of wonderful things happen.'

'Yeah, right. Look, if you're not going to pay up, get lost. And tell the old man the next time I see him, I'm going to shove that broom where the sun doesn't shine.'

'How about if. . .'

'Scram.'

'Yeah, but. . .'

'Look, do I need to come out of here and make you leave?'

Now I'd like to see that, thought Franco, noticing how the scale of the van door and the creature didn't actually match up. 'I was only going to say, how about you give one a try, and if you like what happens, we get our food. If you don't, we say no more about it. What have you got to lose?'

The creature tried not to look interested, but failed. 'Only if I like it?'

'Yup.'

'And I get to decide?'

'Of course.' Franco opened the jar and handed one of the pearls over.

The creature gave it a sniff. 'Doesn't smell minty, right enough. What is it?'

'A Pearl of Nebulus.'

'Pearl, huh? Is it some sort of drug?'

'You could say that.'

'It won't make me go mad or anything, will it?'

'Unlikely.'

'And you say it has wonderful powers?'

'Yup.'

The creature popped the pearl in his mouth and started to sook on it. Nothing happened. Still nothing. Eventually, the creature spat it out. 'Special powers. Right pair of chancers, you are. Go on, get out of here.'

'Your van,' said Franco.

'What about it?'

'It's floating.' And indeed it was. The van was bobbing above the ground, and gently swaying. It also began to softly glow.

'Bloody hell, what have you done?' yelled the creature, starting to panic, as a light breeze caught the van and sent it bobbing higher. 'I tell you, you're not getting any burgers for this. Get me down. Now.'

Franco and the stalblagger tried to grab hold of the van, but it somehow kept slipping through their fingers. Each movement of air seemed to take it higher, until neither of them could even reach the wheels on the bottom.

'Get me down,' the creature shouted, although it was getting harder to hear him. 'Get me down.' The van door opened, but, instead of the creature struggling to get out, a volley of bacon rolls came cascading out.

And the van grew ever smaller, ever higher, ever further away, until it was but a dot on the horizon, and then became a dot you'd be able to see if only the horizon wasn't in the way.

Franco gave a low whistle. 'Did you see that? Makes me

kind of glad it was only my trainers that lit up. A whole van, blimey. Did you know that was going to happen?'

The stalblagger looked at the jar, shook its head thoughtfully, and replaced the spat out pearl.

'Ah well, seems a shame to let these rolls go to waste. Bacon roll, my friend? In fact, take two.' They settled down where they were and began eating.

'God, this roll's got butter in it. I hate butter. Still, the bacon's good. Pity there weren't any cans of juice falling out of the van too.'

'Perhaps I may offer you a cup of tea from my flask.' It was the old man.

The pair nearly choked on their rolls with surprise. 'Bloody hell, where did you spring from?' asked Franco.

The old man smiled. 'That was very clever how you got rid of that dreadful burger van. Tell me, how exactly did you do it?'

'We turned up the thermostat on the deep fat fryer.' Franco looked at the stalblagger to make sure the jar had been hidden away. It had.

'Oh, if only things were ever so simple,' said the old man, smiling. It was clear he was waiting for them to elaborate, but something about his manner was strangely off-putting.

'That's electrics for you,' said Franco.

'Quite, quite.' More smiling.

'Well.' Franco stood up. 'Time we should be heading. C'mon Sparky. Nice to meet you again, and happy sweeping. Sparky, grab a couple more of those rolls for later. Bye then.'

'One last thing.' For an old man with a broom, he seemed

to be able to move awfully fast, too quick to even see him do it, and appeared directly in front of the pair. 'Hand over the jar.' He held out his hand.

'What jar?'

'Come, come. We all know you have it. I saw the van. It takes more than "electrics" to make something glow like that. Only a Pearl of Nebulus can do that.'

'A Pearl of what?'

The old man sighed. 'Don't be silly now. Although. . .' He paused thoughtfully. 'It is possible you don't realise what it is you have in your possession. Which means. . .' He smiled. 'Very good, very good. So sorry to have bothered you. My mistake. Busy, busy. Bye then.' And he was gone.

There was a pause as the air filled in the space where the old man had been.

'Why is it I'm thinking that very good, very good means very bad, very bad?' asked Franco. They both clutched their bacon rolls to them. 'I say we split before Old Man Broom heads our way again.'

And they would have, if their arms hadn't been stuck to their sides, and their feet rooted to the spot.

'I am not in the mood for this,' said Franco. The stalblagger looked similarly unamused. 'It's your fault for accepting that lift from the second mini. If we hadn't got in, we wouldn't have made it to the Buffet, and then we wouldn't have been stuck here like this. Granted, we'd still have been stuck on the surface of this bloody place, but at least we would have had more options, I think. And, admittedly, we might not have got any bacon rolls, but this really sucks.'

The stalblagger wondered if it was worth the risk of the loss of an eyeball, just to get Franco to shut up.

'Hello, hello again. Still here are we?' The old man had reappeared.

'This anything to do with you?' growled Franco.

'Perhaps, perhaps not.' The old man had exchanged his brown coat for a shiny cloak job, the kind magicians who want to appear a bit flash would wear, even if all they can do is make a hat appear out of a rabbit. It was also a bit too long for him, and he made a slight choking noise every time he stood on the edge of it by mistake. 'Now, the Pearls of Nebulus. Which one of you has them?'

'Don't know what you're talking about.'

'Come, come, it was such denials that led to my having to take such measures.'

'Yeah, what exactly did you do to us?'

'Very effective, isn't it? Although it was meant to only immobilise your feet, not your arms as well. Maybe I repeated the words too many times.' He turned, and there was the distinct sound of rustling, as if a book was very quickly being scanned through. 'Hmm. Yes, well. Hmmmm.' A slapping sound, and then he turned back, smiling with a frown. 'No matter. It has served my purpose well. I have got you in my power. The Pearls of Nebulus will be mine. Hand them over.' He held out his hand, and gave a slight choking sound.

'Eh, slight problem there, Merl the Magnificent,' said Franco.

'How do you mean?' The old man readjusted the collar of his cloak.

'We don't have them. They're in the van.'

'What do you mean they're in the van?'

'We didn't have any money on us, so we had to pay in pearls.'

'You paid in pearls? What? What the? Do you realise how much one of those is worth?' The old man's voice began rising towards a screech.

'Well, maybe if someone had paid their own burger bill, we wouldn't be in this position.' Franco tried to point at the old man with his finger to underline his point, but since this was currently impossible, the point got slightly lost.

'You paid in pearls. In pearls!' The old man clutched his imaginary hair in despair. 'In pearls!'

'Yup, and he didn't even give us a discount.'

There was a loud groaning noise, then the old man suddenly leapt forward, arms waving, his face almost as purple as his cloak. 'Do you realise, kkkk, what you've done? Kkkkkk.' The choking was becoming more frequent as he leapt around. 'Do you know how much even one pearl alone is, kkk, worth? And you gave A WHOLE JAR away for some stupid burger!' At this he collapsed sobbing to the ground.

'Sorry,' said Franco. 'I didn't realise it meant so much to you.'

'It meant everything. It was my chance.'

'Although, strictly speaking, they weren't your pearls.'

'What do you mean?' An eye stared out threateningly from amidst the old man's tears, and the sobbing came to a halt.

'Well, far be it from me, finders keepers and all that jazz, ten seconds in the pocket and one in the hand, those pearls were ours.'

The old man got up. 'Kkkk, but they should have been mine, I tell you, mine.'

'Well, it's all kind of academic now really, what with the van and the pearls gone. So, if you could maybe see about undoing this spell of yours, we'll be on our way, seeing as we're not really needed here anymore.'

The old man gave a sigh, and his shoulders drooped. 'Very well. You are of no use to me now.'

'Great, ready when you are.'

'It may take a couple of weeks,' said the old man, looking very dejected.

'A couple of weeks? Are you nuts or something?'

'I need to wait for Part Nine to arrive before I can do anything.'

'Part Nine? Part Nine?' Franco's voice was close to shattering glass.

The old man reached under his cloak and pulled out a deluxe navy and gold binder.

'"*The Complete Wizard*",' read Franco.

The old man flipped open the cover.

Franco read on. '"*The Complete Wizard*. From wand maintenance to world domination in 270 fortnightly parts. Free collapsible wand with Part One."' He looked up. 'Well fan-bloody-tastic. Some bloody magician you are. Bloody cut out and keep abracadabra crap, so it is.'

'Shh,' said the old man, 'you're not supposed to use that one without a certificate.'

'I don't bloody care. And I bet you that bloody cloak of yours came with Part Two.'

The old man didn't reply, suddenly becoming absorbed in an advert on page seven.

Franco took a deep breath. 'Look,' he said slowly, 'is there absolutely nothing you can do without having to wait till the next part comes?'

'I can only work within the confines of my training.' The old man shut the folder and tucked it back under his cloak.

'Training? Training?' Franco was aware his voice was rising again, and quickly dropped it back down. 'Is there no clue or hint in your book at all? Nothing you could use so we don't have to wait till Part Nine comes sauntering along? 'Cause, strictly between you and me, I could do with going for a whiz, and that could be a tad embarrassing in the current situation, if you know what I mean.' He was now speaking so slowly and deeply, whales could have asked him to turn the noise down.

The old man's face went a light shade of pink. 'Oh, oh, indeed, indeed. Hmmm. Well, I really don't know. I could maybe use another spell, see if that has the desired effect, but I'm not really trained in spell substitution. Anything could happen.'

'Anything's got to be better than being stuck here like a couple of dodos.' The stalblagger agreed, although it decided to ask Franco later exactly what a dodo was.

'Well, if you're sure.'

'We're sure, we're sure, aren't we Sparky?'

'Sparky' nodded.

The deluxe gold and navy binder was once more brought out, and the old man began scanning through the pages. 'Unsettable Jelly. That's an idea, although we don't want to loosen you up too much. Hmm. Running Shoes, no, no. Jogging bottoms, dear me no.' More page shuffling. 'Oh no, no, no, well, maybe, yes, well, no, better not.' He looked up. 'It doesn't look like there's anything in here, nothing that would be safe to try. Oh, hold on a minute.' He flicked quickly back. 'Ah, here it is. Yes, yes, this could work very nicely. Hold on while I look at the contraindications. Hmm, hmm. Have either of you recently been near a jam factory?'

They shook their heads.

'Or eaten more than five squares of chocolate within a twenty-four hour period?'

More shaking.

'Well, we should be okay then. Here we go.' He hunched forward slightly, holding the binder in one hand, and holding out the other in a sort of palm down, cramped crab position and intoned, 'Ho, ho, ho, I let you go.' With that, and before they'd had a chance to say anything, Franco and the stalblagger found themselves dashing towards the horizon, then dashing back, after which their legs promptly turned to rubber and they collapsed in a heap on the ground.

'Hmmm, that was somewhat unexpected,' said the old man, bending down to look at them, 'but very interesting. And you say you definitely haven't had any chocolate recently? I must make a note of this,' and began searching in his cloak for a pen.

The pair lay wheezing. Too breathless to speak, the

stalblagger mustered what strength it had to make its eyes glitter like a pair of gold covered chocolate coins hanging in a Christmas tree.

'What the?' croaked Franco.

'No, your friend is quite right,' said the old man, clicking a multi-coloured biro off and on. 'Chocolate coins would also have an effect. You see, chocolate doesn't have to be square to have a desultory result. It can also be circular.'

'Chocolate coins!' croaked Franco. 'We ate chocolate coins!'

'What?' The old man had just selected the purple biro tip and was not best pleased. He hardly ever got to use purple.

'We ate chocolate coins,' repeated Franco, trying to lean up on a rubbery arm unsuccessfully. 'I don't know how long ago that was. Feels like ages. And some fludge, although there was definitely not chocolate in that.' He collapsed back down.

'Well, therein lies your problem. I did ask if you'd had chocolate, and you said no you hadn't. So, I'm sorry, I can't be held responsible for this. Oh no.'

'Not responsible? Listen pal.' Franco tried to look as menacing as he could whilst still resembling a human puddle. 'It was you and your magic spells got us in this predicament in the first place. It wouldn't have mattered if we'd eaten round chocolate or triangular cheese if you hadn't started with your abracadabray whatsit. And once I've figured out how to get us up and off the ground here, me and my pal are off to the newsagent to cancel your subscription, and then you'll just be an eight-part wizard all the rest of your days.'

'You wouldn't dare.' The old man's eyes stared furiously.

'Try me.'

'This is quite intolerable, intolerable I say. I could report you to the Magic Council for this, for reckless interference in a wizard's training and misappropriation of the magic word beginning with A.'

'Yeah, and they'll probably say thank God, we never liked the purple cloaked little twonk in the first place. Thanks for saving us the bother.'

'I have never been so insulted in my life. I've a good mind to. . .'

'To what? Cast a spell on us? Just watch you're not standing on your cloak as you do it or you might actually get it right this time.'

'Why you. . .'

And the argument might well have continued in this vein if, at that moment, the stalblagger hadn't leapt up in the air, whistled like a dog and turned into an elevator.

The doors slid open.

So did Franco's and the old man's mouths.

The doors slid shut.

The mouths stayed where they were. Franco tried to point at the elevator, and the old man tried to nod. Franco nodded in the direction of the magic folder, and the old man shook his head. Then the doors opened once more, this time with a cheery ping. Above the doors was a panel that read 'Up, Down, Somewhere Else', although the arrow that was meant to point to the selected option appeared to be missing. There was a hint of muzak drifting out of the interior, and the merest whiff of bacon rolls.

'After you,' whispered Franco.

The old man's eyes grew wide.

The elevator gave a ping, ping, ping as if to hurry them along.

'It could be a trap,' whispered the old man.

Franco agreed, although he didn't like to say so. After all, what now looked like a lift could suddenly change back into a stalblagger and the implications of that if they were still inside didn't bear thinking about. There was also the issue that what had happened to the stalblagger could also happen to him, although he did slowly seem to be regaining the use of his limbs unaccompanied by any side effects. Still. . .

The elevator began pinging more frantically, and the previously missing indicator arrow, inexplicably mounted on the side, began swinging up and down, as if pointing at something behind them.

Franco looked. There in the distance, revealing the true size of his bulk now it was unconstrained by a burger van, was the burger van creature coming their way, and unsurprisingly enough, he didn't look too happy.

Franco decided that being pummelled into a human patty was less preferable to turning up in the digestive tract of a stalblagger, and wobble-crawled through the doors. 'Let's go, Sparky,' he said.

But the doors stayed resolutely open.

'Don't tell me you're waiting for Old Man Magic over

there. Are you forgetting who got us in this mess in the first place?'

The elevator said nothing.

Franco sighed. 'Okay, you win. But don't blame me if he starts waving his wand around and we all end up inside out with our jumpers over our heads. Hey, Merlin!' Franco raised his voice. 'Are you coming or what?'

The old man turned to look at him, eyes all wide and excited. 'But don't you see? Now is my chance. Now is my opportunity to gain the Pearls of Nebulus and attain the previously unattainable. I will become a Grand Level Three Wizard with extra parking rights. I will be beyond the beyond. I will be. . .'

'Split into tiny pieces and force-fed through a pneumatic meat mincer,' said Franco.

But the old man wasn't listening, preferring to rifle through his pockets for a plastic bag without a hole in the bottom to put the pearls in.

'Your choice. Although I wouldn't like to be in your shoes when he tries removing that meat cleaver from your head.'

It's amazing how attractive a cleaver can look when its blade is shining in the sun, but the beads of perspiration now appearing on the old man's forehead suggested this quality was currently passing him by.

The doors slid shut.

Chapter Six

'And now, destination anywhere,' said Franco. 'Preferably an anywhere that doesn't involve pompoms, burger vans and half-baked wonk wizards. Oops, sorry, I forgot. We're bringing our own with us, aren't we? Whatever crazy looped circuitry put that idea in your brain I'm having removed, just as soon as I'm back out in the open air. And another thing, did you have to eat so many onions with your roll? The stink in here's horrendous. God only knows what the bathroom smells like after you've been. Actually, scratch that last thought and pass me the controls. Let's flick the switch and get moving before Captain Cape here starts getting creative.

'Buttons. Looking for buttons. Not seeing buttons. Ah, there's one, big and shiny. What does that say there? "Don't Press."' Pause. 'Is this your idea of a joke? First you make us wait for the Purple Wonder and now this. What's next? An en-suite paddling pool with optional rubber and go-cart facility? And will you turn that bloody music off. It's doing my head in. Thank you. "Don't Press", it says. "Don't Press." Easiest way to decide this is to throw an imaginary coin.

Heads says I press, tails says I don't. Oh look, it's heads. Better press it then.'

A big rubber hammer came swinging out of the ceiling and clunked Franco on the head.

'I s'pose you think that's funny, do you?' He clutched his head. 'You could have really hurt me there. My skull's not as thick as you think. God, I am so going to chin you when I get out of here.'

There was a second's silence.

'Did you just burp? That's disgusting. You do realise I could get you on health and safety charges, release of noxious substances and all that. That's the last time I let you eat a bacon roll, that's all I'm saying. Now get us moving and out of here before I turn into a peptic ulcer.'

Ping went the doors. 'Thank you for travelling with Internal Elevators.'

'That's just you holding your nose and talking funny,' said Franco. 'You don't fool me. 'Course, I can't speak for the Man in Purple here. Actually, where is Old Man Magic? I can see his cloak but I can't see him. Funny, I don't remember any puff of smoke, so he can't have disappeared.' He picked up the cloak and gave it a little shake. 'Definitely nothing there. Strange. Unless. . .'

He looked up. 'You've gone and bloody eaten him, haven't you? I knew it. That smell isn't burgers. It's burgers in stomach acid. You dissolved him. In fact, I'm sure I'm two inches shorter than when I came in here. You're dissolving me too. Look at the bottom of my trainers. Oh, they're still there. But my arms definitely look thinner, and look at my chest. You're eating me from the inside out. I'm being eaten alive by an elevated stalblagger who thinks the best way to eat a jar of jam is from the bottom up. Still haven't figured out how you do that. Do you use a straw or a very long spoon or something? Anyway, aaargh, I'm being eaten alive by an, oops, repeating myself there. And that's what I hope I'll do to you, keep repeating for a very long time. Because no-one eats Franco Strontium without getting really bad indigestion.'

There was a round of applause.

Franco looked around to see the doors open and a group of fleshy haired little people with smiles on their faces standing there clapping.

'That's all folks. Come back for Part Two when our hero overpowers the gut monster and gives it a right good ticking off. Thank you and goodbye.' Franco pressed a button that definitely hadn't been there before. The doors shut, then opened, then shut again. Then opened.

The smiling faces were still there.

'Sorry folks, we're not going to your floor. Try the stairs.'

There was a ripple of applause as the doors appeared to finally close.

'What the hell happened there? Oh look, someone threw a rose. How thoughtful. But don't think that lets you off the hook. When I get out of here, I'm so going to. . .'

Once more the rubber hammer swung down, this time without the aid of a Don't Press button.

Chapter Seven

'And the funny thing is, he never had a banana on him in the first place. Quite extraordinary, indeed. Your move, I believe.'

Franco raised his head to see the stalblagger and the old man sitting on either side of an upturned crate playing draughts. And were those empty wine gum packets lying there?

'Ah, the sleeper awakes. Good morning there, or, as I believe they say in the Fifth Precinct, wotcha wotcha. Or is it only the one wotcha? No matter, good morning one and all. Although technically,' the old man looked at his watch, 'it has gone afternoon. I don't know what the Fifth Precinct say there. Or even if they have an afternoon. But it's the thought that counts. Ah, I see what you've done,' he said, turning back to the draughtboard. 'Very clever. But all I need to do is, oh, ah, I see. Dear, dear, this will require some thought.'

Franco put his head back down on the ground. Things made more sense there. So, the Purple One hadn't been dissolved in acid after all. Was this a good thing or not? He wasn't sure, although the fact that they hadn't saved him any wine gums suggested it was in the balance. That, and the old man was still clad in purple.

'Your friend appears to have collapsed again. Should we try the cattle prod once more?'

'Whoah, ho, ho. There'll be no cattle prodding round here.' Franco was up and on his feet in less time than it takes a fly. However, a fly, once up, generally tends to stay that way, unless it forgets which way is up. Franco was no fly, and the sudden rise in altitude caused his brain, which was more in a wake up, think about getting up, think again, then consider it frame of mind, to overload and bring him back to a pre-fly feet stage. Plus it had remembered it had a large bump on the top of it which it was still in the huff about. It did, though, allow Franco to give a little stagger first, enabling him to knock into the draughtboard and send the pieces dancing onto the ground.

'And at the very moment I was about to play to win. Hard luck, old chum. Best of fifty?' asked the old man.

Yes, things definitely made more sense at ground level, thought Franco. For a start, all this is probably only happening as a result of the hallucinogenic properties of stomach acid and this is my brain's way of trying to soften the impact of hitting the large intestine, or whatever it is a stalblagger has stuffed up there. Probably a loo brush. God, I'm about to get loo brushed. 'Bring on the stomach acid. I'm about to get high.'

He was suddenly conscious he might have said the last bit out loud, but since it was all a figment of his imagination anyway, it wasn't really a problem. Though the inclusion of the wine gums still really narked him. You'd think his brain would have given him at least one last chortle, like looking up to find the others had been munching on laxative tablets or something. Although where he was going, this would only have rubbed it in. Better to imagine them both with chicken heads or dressed as bananas or something.

He lifted his head to see whether his brain had obliged. All he could see was the old man tutting at having to use mints instead of counters, and the stalblagger eating one when he wasn't looking.

The old man looked at the board, then looked squinty at the stalblagger, then at Franco.

'Don't look at me,' said Franco. 'I'm busy hallucinating.'

The old man looked back at the board, fiddled with his ear, then moved a counter.

Upon which the stalblagger jumped over everything and swallowed the winning piece, which turned out to be a counter rather than a mint, but it didn't seem to be too bothered.

The old man scowled, like one who's still sure he's had a fast one pulled over him, if only he could work out what. 'Hmmph. Yes, well, hmmph,' he said, as the stalblagger shuffled the pieces back into the box and the mints back into the jar. He twitched his foot and tapped his arm with his finger as the board went into the box and the lid went on, held in place by an elastic band. 'Hmmph. Yes, well, I've always been more of a crossword man myself,' he said, and promptly pulled out a word search.

The stalblagger gave the elastic band a ping and then tucked the box away. Then it took out a paper napkin, placed it over its eyes, and lay back for a snooze.

God, this is dull, thought Franco. It's like a hundred Sundays rolled into one, without even the promise of a Horlicks at the end of it. Who would have thought a hallucination could be so boring. He let out a loud sigh, hoping this might give his brain a hint and nudge it into doing something more interesting. Although he didn't hold out much hope. It hadn't ever done anything interesting before.

But then he got a piece of paper thrust under his nose by an unseen hand. Ah ha, he thought, this is more like it. I knew you wouldn't let me down, brain. He looked up to see where the unseen hand had come from, but all he saw was the dozing wrinkly lump of a stalblagger, and an old man looking like a discarded purple chocolate muttering, 'Where is apple? I've already got kumquat. Tsk, tsk,' and tapping a biro on the end of his knee.

Franco sat up to read the note.

'*Dear Franco,*' it began.

So far, so good, thought Franco.

'*You're probably wondering what is going on.*'

Damn right I am.

'*Suffice to say, all information is given on a need to know basis, and you don't need to know.*'

Franco scrunkled up the note in disgust and threw it away. Then he got up and picked it up and stuffed it in his pocket. He didn't want a pompom creature suddenly appearing and ticking him off for littering. Hallucination or not, he wasn't taking any chances.

The note gave a little cough and continued.

'What the. . .'

'*As I was saying. . .*'

Franco checked his pocket for the scrunkled-up paper. Still there. 'How are you doing that?' he asked.

'*Magic,*' said the note.

'No, really, how are you doing it?'

'*Verbal astral spacial reproduction.*'

'Right.'

'*You don't know what that is, do you?*'

'Not really.'

The note gave a sigh, or rather, Franco saw the word '*sigh*' appear in front of his eyes, with an extra emphasis on the 's'. '*Basically, instead of words on a page, VASR.*'

'Doesn't really trip off the tongue, does it?'

'*VASR enables the words to appear directly in front of the reader without the need for any external source.*'

'Right. So, can someone read what you're saying over my shoulder?'

'*Only with a mind tap.*'

'A what?'

'*A mind tap. Because the words are created inside the brain of the reader, they only appear to be in front of the eyes. Thus, the only way to read what someone else is reading is with a mind tap.*'

'And what's one of those?'

'It's a tap that's fitted to the top of the head and used to read the mind.'

'You don't say.'

'Now if we could please return to the main part of the text.'

'Hang on a minute there, pal. You're telling me that all these words appearing in front of me are because you're putting them there?'

'Basically, yes.'

'And what if I don't feel like reading?'

'Look, we really don't have time for this.'

'Oh yes we do. And I haven't even started on the chances of someone sticking a tap on my head. Ouch, ouch, **bold print**. That really hurt.'

'Now will you listen?'

'Do I have a choice? You can't go round using typefaces like that. Someone could really get hurt.'

The note was about to go bold capitals underlined in red, but thought better of it. Were all humans as annoying as this one? Not for the first time it questioned not making the move to the internal post-it note division. At least there any message was usually short and sweet, and often illegible, which led the recipient to mentally throw it away fairly quickly. Although it had heard of notes that went unread and became covered in more notes, until everything became such a jumble of words, the recipient would resort to clearing them all out with a cotton bud and a dose of liver salts. But, it was a job, and right now, more appealing than this one.

It decided that the best approach here was to start relaying the message and pray the human shut up and read. '*All information is on a need to know basis and you don't need to know.*' I've a mind to take you out of my pocket and use you to wipe my concentrate, thought the note.

'Don't you mean need to nose basis?,' said Franco. 'Since you're already up it anyway.'

'*However*,' the note continued, ignoring him, '*it has been agreed a minimum level of information will have to be given in order for you to complete your quest.*'

'Quest? The only quest round here is me stopping myself from entering a stalblagger's internal combustion system any sooner than I have to.'

Don't ask, thought the note. '*You must deliver the packlarge to the. . .*'

'Don't you mean package? Look, it's even highlighted as being wrong.'

Oh shiny bright, thought the note, this one didn't have the latest Interverbal Translation Upgrade. In fact, there were a whole load of bits missing. Nevertheless, there was no time to change that now. It would have to plough on regardless. '*You must deliver the packlarge to the quondrotional arena before the hogwallet is relocated in birectional axis. Then the ballast will be upendidly grandilated and your quest will be complete.*'

'It'd be a whole lot more complete if I understood what you were on about.'

Oh well, thought the note, you can't win them all, and promptly disappeared.

'Hey, where have you gone? What on earth's a quon, quond, qu, and what on earth's that smell?'

He looked down to see a plume of smoke rising from his pocket, accompanied by the smell of singed fabric. Terrific, he thought, I was hoping these trousers would do me till the end of the week. Now they'll need to last a fortnight.

'Ah ha!'

Franco looked round.

'There you are. I knew you could not hide from me forever.' The old man scored out APPLE with a flourish, and triumphantly folded up the word search. Simultaneously, the stalblagger folded away the napkin, and gave a small stretch and a quick armpit scratch.

Franco looked to see if they'd noticed anything of what had just happened, but it appeared not. Best not to mention it, he decided, and walked over, trying to discreetly waft away the last of the smoke.

'Good sleep?' asked the old man.

The stalblagger gave Franco a wink.

Franco, suspicious that reality wasn't all it was cracked up to be, and that this might be reality after all (in which case, that meant he wasn't. . . and he hadn't been. . . and he wasn't going to. . . and those fleshy haired people were. . . and the old man. . .). He chose not to examine the implications of all these occurrences and go for the one fact he could make sense of. 'You hit me,' he said, pointing at the stalblagger.

Who, moi? The stalblagger gave a look of wide eyed

84

innocence, which was only spoilt by a very slight giggle at the end.

'Hard,' said Franco. 'I could sue.' His dander was up and rising.

'I very much doubt it,' interjected the old man, who had begun cleaning his nails. 'You'd have to be a brainwave in order for that to happen. And since we're currently *in loco parenthesis*, that may not be possible. My, my, those nails have got dirty.'

Franco regarded him the same way a goldfish would a tree. Blankly.

'Your friend here decided the best way to get out of our predicament was to hide ourselves in some text, and I must say I agreed. You became an afterthought, your friend became parenthesis incarnate, and I myself opted to be a rather stylish semi-colon. Although it has been pointed out to me that this isn't strictly necessary.' He looked up. 'I hope you don't like playing draughts. We may be stuck here for quite some time and the board only accommodates two players.'

'Wine gums. You ate all the wine gums,' said Franco, and began to sob.

'Oh, oh,' said the old man, suddenly embarrassed. 'I'm sure your friend would let you take his place at the board for a short time. And, well, I'm not sure I wouldn't mind letting you borrow my seat while I stretch my legs for a minute or two.' He stood up and brushed down his knees. 'Ah, this looks like a good direction,' and off he went.

Franco sat down.

'Ah, you wouldn't mind extending the length of the bracket, would you?' called the old man's voice. 'Thank you.'

The stalblagger unfolded its hanky and handed it over to Franco.

'Thanks,' Franco sniffed.

They sat there in silence for a few moments.

Eventually, the stalblagger reached over and patted Franco on the shoulder, then straightened its face as the old man reappeared.

'Very refreshing,' said the old man. 'Ah, still sitting in my seat.'

The stalblagger looked at him.

'No matter. These varicose veins won't be going anywhere, after all.' He shuffled from foot to foot, like an unhappy chocolate wrapper, until the stalblagger got up and covered him in parcel tape, thereby pinning him down. Then it reached into Franco's pocket, took out the note and nodded sagely as it read.

'Hey, how did you do that?'

'Anything is possible in parentheses, provided one uses the correct punctuation.'

'So if I said you were a. . .'

'Exactly. You forgot to use an apostrophe, so the sentence was cancelled.'

'Doesn't explain your accent and that how now brown cow vowel sound.'

'Remember what the old man said. I am parenthesis incarnate. I can choose whatever vowel sound I want.'

'Yeah, but did it have to be that one?'

'Feeling better then, are we?'

'Maybe,' said Franco, and gave an exploratory sniff. He thought for a second, and then said, 'How come I don't get to choose?'

'You're an afterthought, remember? It will only cross your mind to do it once this is over.'

'Right.' Pause. 'I think I preferred it when you were monosyllabic and screechy.'

'We all have our dreams,' said the stalblagger. 'Perhaps now while our erstwhile magician is temporarily under wraps, we can discuss this note you received.'

'What, eh, sorry? Right, the note. The note. How come you managed to read it? The note said it wasn't possible, not without a mind tap. Unless. I always thought that thing on top of your head was a wart.'

'It is.'

'Right.'

'And the wart would need to be on top of your head in order to even be considered a mind tap.'

'Right.'

'Not that it would work in this jurisdiction. Something to do with the polar anomaly.'

'Right.'

'Although, strictly speaking, with an easterly wind on a sunny afternoon, it might be possible.'

'Right.'

'But since we are *in loco parenthesis. . .*'

'I thought you said. . .'

'It's really a whizz bug where it all ends up in the end, if you catch my drift.'

'Not really.'

'But we should return to the note forthwith. Even with a parental flamboyance, I'm afraid my powers are still somewhat limited, rendering the adhesive qualities of the parcel tape highly variable, which means, in modern parlance, he could come unstuck any second, which would be most unf. . .'

'I have a wine gum stuck up my bottom,' yelled Franco.

'I beg your pardon?'

'Right. Finally. Now I've got your attention.'

'Quite.'

'You wanted to talk about the note. You've read it.'

'Not really.'

'What do you mean, not really?'

'My handwriting is not what it once was.'

'Your handwriting?'

'Perhaps you could summarise its contents.'

'But I thought you said you read it.'

'No, I did not. You did. I merely stated that I wished to discuss it.'

'Well, why would you want to discuss it if you don't know what it says? It could be a shopping list for all you know.'

'Even my handwriting is not that bad. I can still write banana, you know.'

'How do you know I'd want to buy a banana? Maybe I'd prefer a kumquat.'

'Spell it.'

'C-O-M-E. . .that's not the point. And anyway it's my shopping list. I can spell come qu, I can spell it anyway I like.'

'But it is not kumquat, K-U-M-Q-U-A-T, is it? It is packlarge. I distinctly read packlarge, and unless your previous supply of chocolate coins has magically reappeared in boundless quantities, I doubt you could afford one.'

'Ah, I know what this is about. You're still sore you didn't get another plane ride, aren't you?'

'It is of no consequence here.'

'Yes, you are. I can see your bottom lip sticking out.'

'No it is not.'

'How would you know? Are you a mirror as well as a moron?'

'I beg your pardon?'

'Granted.'

'What?' The stalblagger pulled itself up to its full height. 'I don't think you fully grasp. . .'

'My, my, what's happening here?' asked the old man.

Without turning round, the stalblagger grabbed the tape dispenser and stuck the old man back down again. 'You will tell me of what the note spoke, or believe me, I will. . .'

'You will what? Double bracket me and shove me in the next paragraph? I'd like to see you try.'

'Oh would you?'

'Yeah.'

'Yeah?'

The creature from the van's meat cleaver glinted once more in the sun as it came whizzing past the pair.

'Just a thought,' said Franco, 'but does hiding yourself in some text still work if the other person can't read?' and passed out.

Chapter Eight

Franco decided that maybe fainting wasn't the wisest move in the circumstances and instead lifted his head, just as the cleaver came whizzing past and embedded itself deep in the ground. Franco stared, knowing that even his skull would have a hard time bouncing that one back.

'Nnnnngh.' The creature from the van tried to pull the cleaver back out, but it was resolutely stuck.

'Maybe you should try standing with your feet further apart,' said Franco.

The creature shot him an evil glare.

'Just a thought,' said Franco.

'Right, I'm going to get at least one of you jokers for busting up me and my van, even if I have to use my bare hands.'

'You don't look very busted up to me,' said Franco.

'I'm a quick healer,' growled the creature, 'and you've just gone to the front of the bust up queue yourself. So stay there while I get ready to bash you into a pulp.'

'Scrabble anyone?' The old man was waving around a scrabble set he'd somehow produced from under his cloak.

'Huh?' The creature looked at him.

'Come on, Craven. Remember how well you did the last time? That three letter score was a mighty word indeed. Maybe we can even play it on the board this time.'

'Not now, old man. I've got business to settle first. And don't think I've forgotten about you and your bill. You still owe me, remember? And it was you who sent those jokers to me in the first place.'

'Plenty of time for all of that,' smiled the old man. 'I'm most curious to see if you can manage a four letter word this time.'

'I would have last time if you'd let me spell cat with two Ts,' grumbled Craven.

'Not in the dictionary now, was it? Nor was bus with a U or frog with three legs. All ready when you are.'

'Don't think I haven't forgotten,' said Craven, pointing at the old man, and then sitting down. 'How many letters do I take?'

'Seven.'

'Uh, right.'

'I've already picked some for you. Look, here they are.'

'Thanks.'

'Oh look, you've got a Z. That's already worth ten points.'

Craven beamed. 'I am gonna thrash your ass, old man.'

'And indeed, I return the challenge to you. Let the contest begin.'

Two hours later, and the first of the letters had yet to be placed.

'Oh for God's sake,' cried Franco in exasperation. 'Dog.

D-A-W-G. Dog. Look, the letters are already in the right order, and it's a triple letter score.'

Craven looked up. 'Are you sure?'

''Course I'm sure. You're using three letters plus an extra one, so that's a triple letter score plus a bonus. And if you put it in the top left hand corner, you can block him from using your double U.'

'Ha! Read 'em and weep, old man.' Craven put the letters down with a flourish, and then sat back, arms folded across his considerable chest.

The old man was about to see if it was possible to spell a word off-board, when a tut came from Dictionary Corner.

They all looked round to see the stalblagger sitting on top of the most enormous dictionary, whilst flicking through a teeny tiny pocket version, which, as everyone knows, is much more reliable and only contains the words you really need. And, apparently, D-A-W-G wasn't one of them.

'Let me see that,' said Franco.

The stalblagger carefully pointed to where the word should have been, had it been there.

'Bollocks,' said Franco.

The old man sniggered.

Craven looked to see if he had the letters for that, then realised he didn't know how to spell it.

'How about wagged? W-A-G-D. That must be in there,' said Franco.

The old man sniggered again, but the stalblagger held up a just-a-minute finger, before perusing the pages.

W-A-G-D was allowed.

'I don't believe it,' said the old man. 'Let me see that.' He snatched the book, handing it back when he realised he had the wrong pair of reading glasses on.

'Does that mean I've won?' asked Craven.

'You betcha,' said Franco. 'And the winner gets to buy everyone else an ice-cream. Look, there goes the ice-cream van now. If you're quick, you can catch it. And remember, a big flake in mine, but easy on the strawberry sauce.'

Craven pounded off towards the horizon.

'Right, now that we've got rid of Burger Boy, I suggest we vamoose out of here before Champion the Wonder Flake comes bouncing back. Oh, an ice-cream with an extra-large flake and just enough strawberry sauce. Eh, thanks.'

'And a choc dip ice-cream sandwich,' said Craven, handing it to the old man. 'Mint flavour.'

The old man couldn't get hold of it quick enough.

'And they were all out of strawberry wobbles, so I got you a cherry sundae surprise instead. Hope that's okay.'

The stalblagger beamed in delight.

'Did you not get anything for yourself, young Craven?' asked the old man, once he'd got over the first minty rush.

'Naw,' said Craven. 'The glory of winning was enough for me. I can't wait 'til the next time I see my cousin. He said I'd never amount to anything. It's his van you smashed, by the way. Just thought you ought to know.'

'And is he as handy with a meat cleaver as you are?' asked Franco, halfway between trying to decide whether to eat the flake and try to keep the flaky hole there, or whether to keep pushing the flake down as he ate and see if he could

94

work it all the way down the cone without shattering it and getting it all over himself, as usually happened.

'Naw,' said Craven. 'Not since his mum banned him from playing with anything sharp.'

'That's reassuring,' said Franco, and picked the remains of the ice-cream off his shirt.

'So guys, what do we do next?' continued Craven.

'We? I didn't know there was a "we".'

'Yeah, 'course there is: you, me, him and, eh, it. Sorry, hard to tell.'

The stalblagger shrugged calmly. It could forgive just about anything for a cherry sundae surprise.

'And since I've lost my job, I thought I could hang out with you guys and we could, y'know, do something.'

'Do something?' Franco was dumbfounded. 'Not that long ago you were trying to split open our heads with a meat cleaver, and now you want to hang out with us?'

'Is that a problem?'

''Course not. I love hanging out with folks with a taste for sharp shiny objects and vanilla ice-cream. Nothing I like more. In fact, I was only saying earlier what a shame it is there aren't more meat cleaving and dairy dessert combos around. 'Cause, y'know, there's nothing quite like having your life flash before your eyes to give you an appetite for ice-cream.'

'Is that a yes?'

''Course it's not a yes. Are you nuts or something? If it was a yes I'd be smiling and nodding, not frowning and trying not to choke on what was, admittedly, a very nice

95

vanilla cone. "Is that a yes." You know, you'd think with a head that size there'd at least be something in it. What the. . .'

The stalblagger knew it would later regret the loss of the remaining sundae, but sometimes these things had to be done.

Craven looked puzzled. 'I don't understand.'

'Do not worry there, my friend,' said the old man. 'As my other friend in the wrinkly suit' (the stalblagger raised an eyebrow at this remark) 'has so eloquently put it, welcome to the team.'

'What about him?' Craven pointed at Franco.

'Ah yes, lactose conglomerant, I'm afraid. He'll be fine in a moment.'

Craven smiled broadly. 'Great. I've never been in a team before.'

'No? Well, welcome aboard, and welcome aboard again – or is that once more? – my friend. My associate will organise you a name badge and then we can be on our way.'

'Where will we be going?'

'Ah well, indeed, you see, as part of a team you will be involved in that decision, although any final decision falls to myself, being, as I am, the most qualified amongst us.'

'Qualified?'

'You are looking at an eight-part wizard,' said the old man, striking a suitably magical pose. 'Khhh.'

Craven wasn't sure what that meant and looked over to the stalblagger for a clue. But, as the stalblagger was busy with a Bows & Buttons™ Portable Badge Maker (Make Buttons, Make Friends™) he was on his own, and so tried to pull what felt like a duly impressed face. Qualifications were good, weren't they?

'I see you are highly impressed,' said the old man.

Must remember that face, thought Craven. Use it the next time Granny does her trick with the false teeth, instead of being sick in the lemonade.

'Ah, your badge. Delightful. And one for me too. How kind. What does it say? Only it's too close for me to read now you've pinned it on. Oh, you can't read it either. It's also too close for you. Ah dear, the curse of farsightedness, I know it well. But we can still admire the pretty colours, and what pretty colours they are, my, my. In fact. . .'

The stalblagger started rummaging for the loo brush, then thought better of it, and started picking its nose instead.

'My mother used to say how good I looked in colours as a child, especially. . .'

'Cherry,' said Franco, wiping his mouth.

The old man scowled. 'I was going to say autumn sunset viridian, on account of my delicate complexion. I would prefer it if you. . .'

'I don't usually like cherry, but that sundae's alright, isn't it?'

'Would you please allow me to talk? I was trying to share with your associates the. . .'

'My what?'

It was at this point the stalblagger decided that even something as intricate as an impacted bogey extraction would not create enough distraction from the situation at hand, and since it had only packed the one loo brush, its best recourse was another sook of a mint. After all, nothing detrimental had happened the last time, only a temporary ability to cheat at draughts and to tune out any voice above Level Five on the Whine-O-Meter.

'So, what's this we're looking at?'

The stalblagger looked round with more than a little surprise and disappointment. It had been enjoying the effect the mint had created of enabling it to watch the whole scenario as if looking into a glass bubble, an out of bubble experience, as it were, and one that thoughtfully came without sound. What it hadn't anticipated was to have to share this time out with anyone.

'God, my hair's a mess,' said Franco. 'It looks like it's had a fight with a packed lunch, and the packed lunch won. Is that dandruff on your shoulders?'

No, the stalblagger hadn't anticipated it at all. It gave a sigh of resignation, and stared at the scene below.

They both stared, watching what appeared to be a heated discussion about hopscotch between Craven and the old man, judging by the amount of hopping and use of chalk that was going on.

'Isn't it funny being able to watch yourself even though yourself doesn't know that you're watching? I wonder what myself would say to me if myself knew what I was doing? Hold that thought, I'm off for a dump.'

The stalblagger said nothing, continuing to stare into the bubble as if coloured squares and hopping were as fascinating as they didn't appear to be. Oh look, someone had started using purple chalk. It had to be the old man. It was. Oh joy. Sigh.

There was the sound of copious amounts of toilet roll being unfurled, followed by a long flush, then another.

Franco reappeared, shaking one leg. 'God, that's better isn't it? You always feel better after a good dump, eh?'

The stalblagger tried to will his miniature bubble self to give miniature bubble Franco a swift kick, or at least nick his chalk when he wasn't looking.

'Hey! Are you trying to kick me there? Look!' Franco jabbed his finger at the bubble, which responded by bursting. 'Oh, was that meant to happen? Have you got another one on you? No? Oh, right. Oh well, never mind. It was all getting a bit boring anyway. I mean, what kind of eejit puts letters in a hopscotch box? That's asking for trouble. C'mon, I fancy a pint.'

Pointy elbows and a deft hand with a packet of crisps meant that they were soon sitting at a corner table in a busy pub, pints of something or other frothing in front of them, the something apparently trying to climb out of the glasses, and surrounded by the type of creatures the stalblagger had never seen outside of an A-Z, but if it had it was pretty sure it would never have planned to share a pub or any other sort of drinking establishment with them. At least none of them had used its head as target practice. At least none of them had used its head more than once for target practice. More than twice. Three times. It stuck a coffee cup on its head, and that seemed to put them off.

Franco appeared not to notice anything, being so much lower than the other clientele and hard to see in the crowd, although someone had temporarily tried to use him as a table, till they discovered their glass kept emptying without them drinking any of it. As a result Franco was ahead of the stalblagger by two or three drinks, and making as much sense as one. 'So, you see, I thought he was saying save your sister, but in fact he was asking if I wanted salt and vinegar. Classic, eh? I mean, you couldn't make it up, could you? C'mon, drink up. We're out of here.'

The stalblagger watched its drink finally make it out of the glass and start slithering across the table, a faint green glow emanating off it. The pineapple chunks and little paper umbrella that had also been in the glass seemed to be going with it, although the cocktail stick on the umbrella looked as though it could be a little tricky if the drink decided to negotiate the hessian wallpaper.

The stalblagger helpfully removed it, and got a pineapple chunk in the eye for its trouble.

The next pub looked vaguely similar to the first, only noisier, and with a table that wobbled. Every time the table wobbled, the stalblagger's drink gave a shriek and then berated it in some strange foreign language.

'My drink's talking to me,' said the stalblagger.

'Yeah, mine usually does that after two or three. Wait till it tries getting out of your glass, then you'll know you're really drunk, or is it meant to do that? I can never remember. Anyhoo, what, way, what was I saying? Aw aye, the juggernaut was going straight for my head and I said, I says hey, you.'

The stalblagger let the wall do the listening for it and instead concentrated on gathering enough drink mats to get rid of the wobble. Finally, it was able to have its drink in peace. Well, almost.

'Packlarge for Strontium. Packlarge for Strontium.'

'Is that me? Aye, that's me. Hold on a minute there, pal. Be back with you in a sec.' Franco gave the wall an affectionate pat. 'Aye pal, hey, that's me,' he called out.

'You Strontium? Sign here.' A courier with a bright orange baseball cap and a look that suggested that that was the brightest thing about him pushed through the crowd. 'Sign here. And here. No, the next one. Great. Enjoy.'

A brown paper parcel with the word PACKLARGE printed on the front in red capitals was thrust Franco's way.

'Oh goody, is that for me?' said Franco, then stared at it like he was trying to figure out what should happen next.

The stalblagger gently pulled the string wrapped around it.

'Hey, get away. It's my parcel. Oh, look, a book! Isn't that. . . what the hell am I meant to do with a book? A book. Well, there's no way I'm carrying that around with me all night. I mean, do I look like a walking bookcase? Don't answer that. Oh, it's starting to glow. Why's it starting to glow? Hey, Sparky, why's it doing that?'

Apparently Franco wasn't the only one wondering why, as now the whole pub was watching them, and seemed to be waiting for an answer.

'I think we'd better go,' said the stalblagger, quietly covering its drink so as not to be interrupted by it.

'Go? I'm not going. I haven't finished my drink, and anyway, I can't move under the weight of this book that won't stop bloody glowing.'

The stalblagger covered its glass with a mat and gave it a really good shake. This caused the drink to shriek so loudly all the glasses in the place shattered, meaning everyone was crawling around, trying to stop their drinks from escaping.

'Now!' said the stalblagger, grabbing both Franco and the book under its arm and nimbly running over the backs of the other customers and out the door.

'Name.'

'Franco Stontium.'

'Is that with one "N" or two?'

'One.'

'And you, Sir?'

'That's Spakee.'

'I'd rather the, I'd rather it, I'd. . . Quiet sir, while I ask your. . .'

'It's Grubber,' said the stalblagger.

'Nice one,' whispered Franco loudly, and gave the stalblagger a nudge.

'Is he usually like this?' The police officer tilted his head in the direction of Franco.

Grubber's face said it all, so the officer wrote it down, just in case. 'So, gentlemen,' he glanced again at the notebook. "*Barrel of monkeys*" it read. 'You do realise you were running whilst carrying a book, don't you?'

'So-ae offisa. Won' 'appen again, offisa,' said Franco.

The offisa, sorry, officer was beginning to understand the monkey reference now. 'Only, you could have someone's eye out with that. Do you realise how many book-related injuries there were last year? A creased spine is no laughing matter.'

Franco sniggered.

'Just treat your books with more respect in the future, or next time you might not get off so easily and I'll be forced to paperclip you.'

Grubber nodded sagely.

'Well, on your way now gentlemen, before I change my mind. Incidentally, does it always glow like that?'

Grubber nodded parsley as he had run out of sage.

'Well I'll be. And I thought I'd seen most things. A glowing book, huh. 'Night, gentlemen.' And with that he packed up his tentacles and rolled away.

Franco would have probably sniggered again at this point, if he hadn't already nodded off, nestled as he was against the stalblagger.

Grubber gently picked him up, slung him in a fishing net over his shoulder, and walked off to find a bench somewhere quiet to sit and have a read of the book.

Chapter Nine

Once Grubber had persuaded a pink eyed do-gooder that the bench was not safe to sit on, mainly through the medium of hand puppetry, he sat down, flicked on the standard lamp next to it, and began to read. He'd got to the part where. . .

'Aargh, help, help, I've been spidered.'

Instinctively, the stalblagger reached for the hairspray, before remembering who was in the net, then reached for it anyway. Then thought better of it, and tipped Franco out.

'Thank God for that. I thought for a minute I was trapped inside some kind of arachnophoidal nightmare or something. I mean, what size would a spider have to be to spin something that size? It'd have to be a right massive son of a beast, and even I know they don't come that. . .'

'Evening.' A massive son of a beast came strolling past and tipped its hat at them.

'Evening,' said Franco and Grubber.

'So, what's that you're reading?' asked Franco, trying to read the cover.

'*The Pearls of Nebulus,*' said Grubber, trying not to lose his place.

'Who wrote that?'

'Bessie White.'

'Any good?'

'It's alright.'

'How much have you got to go?'

'Not much.'

'Can I have a look?' Or, at least, that's what Franco might have said if he hadn't found himself tucking into an orange.

'Hmm.' The stalblagger kept reading.

'I said that sounds fa. . .' The orang-utan with side salad and butternut medley took slightly longer to chew, but not as long as the leather sofa with matching footstool. 'Any more of that butternut stuff? Although I won't be needing another sofa for a while. Those things don't half fill you up.' Franco paused for a burp.

The stalblagger struggled on with the book.

'Funny, that's not the first time I've been spidered, y'know.'

And gave up. Grubber then reached for the emergency bell jar, which should only be used in an emergency, hence the name, and popped it over Franco. And so he was then able to return to the story in peace, only pausing to pop a cover over the jar when Franco's face got too distracting. Then he closed the book with a satisfied thump, tucked it behind his head as a pillow, and turned out the light.

Chapter Ten

In a small little galaxy, far, far away, a little old lady with white hair and a penchant for bovver boots, sat down to write a grocery list. Once again the boots had eaten her out of house and home, and now the cupboard was bare, never mind the lack of a house.

She tried to concentrate on exactly how many tins of tuna were too many, but it wasn't easy with the chilly wind whipping round her ankles. She pulled her scarf a little tighter, scored out *tuna* and wrote *beer*, stuck the whole thing in an envelope and posted it. It was only once the list was published instead of the book that she realised her error.

Sod it, she thought, and reached for the toilet paper.

Chapter Eleven

'And another thing, that's not how you spell it anyway, especially if you're using purple chalk and your pants are on fire.'

'But my pants aren't aay, aaay, aaay.' The old man hastily sat down in an opportunely placed paddling pool. There was the faint sound of hissing and not a little steam.

'And anyway, it's not your turn. It's Craven's. Craven, hey, what the. . . ! Look, how many times have I told you, no drawing on the grid until the game's over.' Franco was livid.

'But I like cats,' said Craven.

'Yeah, and I like handmade bananas, but you don't see me drawing them everywhere, do you? Now go and sit next to Liar Liar Man over there and don't move until I say so. Strewth, bloody amateurs. Where's the chalk? Was that a B or a C there, or a number 1?'

'But my pants aren't. . .'

'Sit.'

So Craven sat with a small splash.

The stalblagger sat up and tucked away his hardback pillow.

'And as for you,' Franco pointed an accusing chalky finger at Grubber, 'going off like that and leaving me to do all the work. Do you know how many times I've had to do this? Exactly. And what am I having to do? Fix it again, 'cause you won't keep an eye on Mr Colour By Numbers and Catboy over there.'

The stalblagger handed the dastardly duo a hairdryer, and quietly packed the paddling pool away.

'Sometimes I don't know why I bother. Sometimes I wish I'd stayed exactly where I'd been and not bothered getting somewhere,' said Franco. He stood up and pointed indiscriminately at them all. 'You know, egg for breakfast isn't so bad if you've had chicken for tea, and that's a fact. But what do I get? Bloody chicken omelette, that's what. With onion. I tell you, if it wasn't for the fact I haven't the slightest idea what I'm talking about, I'd be out of here and dancing along the freeway of ill-begotten bacon sandwiches, so I would. Yes, mark my words, a fatality worse than death is like a fart in an ice-cream: you want to eat it but you know something isn't quite right.' He turned away again, muttering, and started rubbing at another corner of the hopscotch grid.

'Hallucinogenic chalk,' sniggered the old man quietly to the stalblagger. 'Naughty, indeed, but such fun. Although the effect is somewhat stronger than I anticipated. The self-lighting pants for one thing.'

'Yeah, and I hate cats,' muttered Craven.

The stalblagger raised an eyebrow, but not before Franco had spun around on the spot, turned himself into a rainbow, and curled up asleep on the ground.

'Ah, the effects appear to have worn off now,' said the old man. 'We'd better move him out of the way so the next lot can play. There you go, gentlemen. The grid is all yours. Would you like to use our chalk?'

'No, we've got our own,' said a troll, turning himself blue and rolling across the grid at speed. 'Game on!'

The group had to quickly get out of the way as eleven high speed multi-coloured rolling trolls came rushing past.

'Time for some gentle repast, I think. I highly recommend a little bistro on the Flu de Pompet. The waiters know me there.'

But the stalblagger and Craven were already sitting under a striped parasol at a plastic table, signalling to the waitress.

'Or indeed, Patsy's Pizza Parlour. For who would choose fricasseed flambert in a belangesse sauce when one could experience the delights of, what does that say there? Ah yes, Barfino Pizza, "the pizza that won't stay down". Em, just a glass of water for me, thank you, my dear.'

There was a thump from under the table, and a bleary eyed post-rainbowed Franco appeared. The stalblagger helped him into a seat. 'God, I feel awful. Some game, eh? Where are we?'

'A pizza restaurant,' said the old man. 'I believe the others have ordered on your behalf.'

'Great,' said Franco, as a double battered, thin and crispy, this way up was slid in front of him. 'Ha, ha, this way up going down. Oh em, coming back up again. Back in a mo,' and off he dashed.

Eventually, he returned to the table more slowly but less green of face. 'Mind if I have a sip of your water? Thanks.'

At this, the old man disappeared.

'Blimey. Was it something I said?'

'Happens all the time,' said the waitress, who happened to be passing the table at that very moment. 'Someone's finally straightened out the timeline indicator. Well, that bit of it anyway. He'll have gone back to where he's supposed to be, wherever that is. It's usually less far than you'd think.'

Seeing the blank look on Franco's face, she leant forward and said, 'He's your antimaterial lobbybobby, you know, your astral reflection; like you, but the other way round. You think you're two different people, but you both end up reaching for the same thing. In this case, a glass of water. And sorry love, you also should have disappeared.'

'Should I?' asked Craven. 'Guess I should have, shouldn't I? Nice meeting you,' he said to the stalblagger. 'Say hello the next time you brush your teeth.' And with that, he was gone.

'Now can I get you gentlemen anything else? No? Here's the bill then.'

Franco sniffed. 'Load of old bollocks,' he said, once the waitress was out of earshot. 'Still, I won't be brushing my teeth anywhere near a mirror. Just in case, you understand. What's that you're reading?'

'*The Pearls of Nebulus*.'

'Any good?'

'S'all right.'

'Let's have a swatch. "Two bottles lemonade, three bottles

bleach, one pack indigestion tablets." Are you sure it's a book? Reads more like a shopping list.'

'It is.'

'Why are you reading a shopping list?'

'I find it interesting.'

'Doesn't take much to rock your boat, does it? I bet you can't wait till Chapter Two to see if they've decided to get twenty jars of pickled eggs and a razor. You know, I'm beginning to question your idea of entertainment. You're really going to read some old biddy's shopping list?'

'Insights of immense value can be gained from the seemingly mundane.'

'If you say so. Personally, I'd rather take a risk with the incredibly interesting. Actually, I might take a risk with a cup of coffee. I'm not feeling nearly so queasy. Where's that waitress? In fact, where's anything?'

The whole background had gone multi-coloured and swirly, not a Patsy or a pizza to be seen. Although they were both still sat at the plastic table, minus the parasol.

'Hello Grubber,' said a booming disembodied voice.

'Hello Uncle Bob.'

'What the. . . what. . . eh? Who's who? Who's. . . ? And who's. . . ?'

'It's Uncle Bob,' beamed Grubber.

'What's who?'

'I'm who,' said the stalblagger, 'and this is Uncle Bob.'

'Hello,' boomed Uncle Bob.

'Is this some kind of joke?' asked Franco.

111

'No joke,' boomed Uncle Bob. I wanted to see how my nephew was getting on with the book. Any good, nephew?'

'What? Not you too? Does it run in the family or something, reading shopping lists? Not that you're family anyway since I made you up.'

'Ha, ha, ha,' boomed Uncle Bob. 'Now then, which part are you up to?'

'The three for two mousetrap and shampoo set,' said Grubber.

'Ah yes. That one's a bit of a surprise. I thought they'd stopped making those years ago. Don't rush it though. Remember to leave room for Chapter Two.'

'I will, Uncle Bob.'

'Good stuff. Well, bye then.'

'Bye Uncle Bob.'

'You finished with those plates?' The waitress had reappeared, along with everything else.

Since Franco seemed to have lost the power of speech, still coming to terms as he was with the entity that is Uncle Bob, the stalblagger answered for him and gave a nod, then shut Franco's jaw to stop him drooling. As recovery was clearly going to take some time, the stalblagger got out the book again and began reading, when. . .

'Water,' croaked Franco.

The stalblagger handed him some water. Franco drank. 'More water.'

The stalblagger handed him a goldfish. Franco spluttered.

'Pff, pfff, eww. What the. . . ? Ewww,' and swallowed it anyway.

'Water,' said the goldfish, and Franco obligingly drank another glass.

'What's that you're reading?' he asked, once the goldfish had had enough.

'*The Pearls of Nebulus.*'

'Any good?'

'It's all right.'

Franco looked thoughtful for a moment. 'Have we had this conversation before?'

'You have.'

'I have?'

'Yes.'

'But you haven't?'

'No.'

'Fair enough.' He had another think. 'Did I say anything particularly insightful or interesting?'

'Not really.'

'No?'

'No.'

'Oh. Oh well.' He paused for thought. 'Are you trying to read?'

'Yes.'

'Do you want me to shut up then?'

'Yes please.'

'No problem.'

'Okay.'

'How long will you be?'

'Finished.'

'What? Already?'

'Are you folks nearly done? Only I'm starting to clear up now. Oh, a glowing book. Haven't seen one of those for a while. Last time I saw one here, it was some little guy; planning to take over the world, he was. Old chap, purple cloak. Do you know him?' The waitress was back.

'No,' they replied simultaneously.

'Pity,' she said. 'He never paid his bill.' As she began tidying away all the tables and chairs around them, the stalblagger opened the book to Chapter Two ('You've been diddled, mate. Someone's cut a great big hole in your book,' said Franco), and pulled out the little jar of not actually mints ('Good idea, freshen the old breath'), and put them inside the book, upon which the book slammed shut, gave a little cough, and turned out the light.

Chapter Twelve

'It's dark,' said Franco.

'Someone had better put the light on fast so I can put away the last of these tables,' said the waitress.

There was a click, and, lo, there was light. Well, the kind of light you get from a twenty-watt light bulb in a cupboard. So no imagination required there then.

In the cupboard were the stalblagger, Franco and the waitress.

'I haven't got time to be sitting round here. I've got clearing up to do,' said the waitress.

'Of course, madam,' said the book.

'Thank you,' said the now disembodied voice of the waitress, and she was gone.

The book sat self-importantly in the middle of the table. Ah yes, a table, a stalblagger, Franco, and a twenty-watt light bulb, all together in a cupboard. With a book. A talking, glowing book. You get the picture.

'Okay. Now I'm stuck in a cupboard with a talking book and a stalblagger that hasn't changed its skin for over a fortnight.' Franco had also got the picture. 'Come back, Uncle Bob, all is forgiven.'

The book coughed.

'You shouldn't be coughing with that jar of mints inside you,' said Franco. 'Have a sook on one of them. That'll sort you out.'

'You shouldn't go sooking the Pearls of Nebulus on a whim. Not like some I could mention.' If the book had been hoping to make the stalblagger and Franco feel guilty, it had failed miserably. So it tried to look menacing the way only a hardback can.

Franco sniggered. The stalblagger gave a little giggle.

The book wilted slightly, but rallied when it remembered it was the only one who knew where the light switch was. 'I want you to listen here,' it continued.

'No thanks,' said Franco. 'I think I'll wait till you come out in paperback.'

'What?' The book was puzzled.

'I've had enough of notelets and text appearing before my eyes and telling me what to do. So if you think I'm going to listen to some jumped up notepad, you're wrong.'

'But I am the Packlarge.'

'Yeah, and I'm the Third Donkey from the Right, but you don't hear me boasting about it.'

This was a new one for the book. Maybe some of the rules had changed; it had been out of print for a while. No, best to stick to what it knew and worry about any changes later. 'I must be delivered,' it said firmly.

'Well, slap a couple of stamps on your backside and go post yourself.'

The book was thoroughly confused now. 'But I sent you a note.'

'A note? What note?'

'A note saying I must be delivered to the quondrotional arena. Didn't you get it?'

'Oh, that note,' said Franco, having no idea what the book was talking about but feeling he'd better humour it before it sent mints scattering everywhere. 'Didn't read it.'

The stalblagger gave Franco a nudge and pointed at his burnt pocket.

The cogs of a brain can turn very slowly, but eventually the penny came tumbling down the chute of remembrance. 'My pocket!' cried Franco, catching it, and wondering why he was holding a penny in his hand. 'That note! The text in my head! Do you know how long I had a headache for after that? That long!' He held out his arms to demonstrate, but ran out of cupboard space. 'And I still get flashbacks. Or maybe that's the psycho chalk. Who knows? But whatever, it's really. . .'

The stalblagger held up a little sign, while Franco rambled on. It said *'Don't worry about him. He'll stop in a minute. If not, I have an orange with me.'*

Franco stopped, although the stalblagger wasn't sure whether it was because he'd also read the sign.

'So,' said Franco, glancing over at the stalblagger, 'how much for delivery?'

'There is no fee involved,' said the book, relieved to be

back on message. 'But your name will go down in the annals of history, possibly, or at least part of a song.'

'Oooh, hold me back.'

'Is that a yes?'

'Seems I don't have much choice if I. . .' The stalblagger nudged him. 'I mean, if we want to get out of this cupboard.'

'That's what I wanted to hear,' said the book, and sent them all tumbling down a chute back into the broogle mines.

Chapter Thirteen

'Hup, hup, hup, hup.'

Franco and Grubber appeared to be part of some kind of marching convoy, complete with pickaxes over their shoulders and hobbly-nobbly boots.

'Fan-bloody-tastic,' growled Franco. 'Is this your idea of a joke? 'Cause I ain't bloody laughing.'

The book was in no position to be laughing either, having turned into an ordinary book with flippy-floppy pages and everything.

'That's the last time I trust anything a book says. All that grief it gave us and look where it's got us: right back where we bloody started.'

But the stalblagger was too busy concentrating on walking in its hobbly-nobbly boots without falling over to really pay him much attention.

'Are you listening there?'

Grubber tripped, stumbling into the creature in front and sending a ripple through the ranks.

'Watch it!'

Franco and Grubber watched it, as a bulk monster

surveyed the ranks for the source of the trouble. Grubber tucked away the book.

'Don't suppose you've still got that clipboard on you, do you?' whispered Franco, once the bulk monster had passed.

The stalblagger shook his head.

'Damn. Well, maybe we can bargain ourselves a way out of here with those pearls.' Pause. 'It wasn't the mints you gave that book, was it?'

They marched along in silence for a while. Well, in verbal silence at least.

'Well,' said Franco, finally. 'There's nothing else for it as far as I can see, except to pretend to be a couple of statues and hope that someone moves us out of the way.'

'Who left these statues here?' yelled a bulk monster. 'I'm fed up moving statues out of the way. Beats me why they always seem to get left in the middle of a corridor,' he grumbled, humphing the pair into an alcove, turning on the display light, and walking off.

There was a whirring, clicking sound, like gears slotting into place, and the base of the alcove began to rise, taking our two statues with it, up towards the source of the light.

They appeared to have interrupted some kind of mid-afternoon tea. Two men and an older lady were gathered around the remains of various plates of sandwiches and a particularly fine Victoria Sponge in a huge white room. It was hard to discern the true proportions of the room because of the white light which emanated all around, giving everything a fuzzy glow.

'I once thought of knitting a pair of socks, of having the sensual pleasure of feeling the wool run through my fingers, as an external validation of the creative process. But I discovered it's preferable to loop the wool in my mind, and I never drop a stitch,' said one of the men.

They all laughed as heartily as politeness would allow. One slightly overstepped the mark and had difficulty swallowing the last of his Battenberg.

Then they noticed the new arrivals.

'I'm sorry, can I help you?' asked the older woman, eyebrows raising.

'Em, which way are the toilets?' asked Franco.

'Over there,' said the older woman, pointing into the vague whiteness.

'Thanks,' said Franco, walking as if he was perfectly used to walking into blurry white conditions with no idea of where he was going. And the man who had previously choked on the Battenberg reached for another cup of tea.

'Toilet' said a little brass panel in a near invisible white door. Franco fumbled for the hard-to-see handle. Two white doors sat on the other side of the first door. Neither indicated their purpose, and both were locked.

'Well, that's Jim Dandy,' he said, and realised there wasn't anybody behind him to hear him. Not sure what to do next, Franco went back through the first door, shaking his hands like someone who could have done with leaving them a couple more seconds under the hand dryer but couldn't be bothered.

He saw the stalblagger sitting at the table with the others, apparently sharing a virtual knitting pattern with the older woman.

'Um,' said Franco, wandering over. He pulled out a chair and sat down, which didn't appear to raise any objections.

'Sandwich?' asked one of the men. 'Most of the ham and relish ones have gone, but the roast chicken is also very nice.'

'Eh, thanks,' said Franco.

'Tea? It's gone cold, I'm afraid, but still refreshing.'

'We had hoped you were bringing a fresh pot when you arrived,' said the other man.

'Right,' said Franco. 'Sorry about that.'

'No need,' said the first. 'I'm sure they'll be along shortly.'

The stalblagger and the older woman gave a laugh at a particularly humorous combination of knit and purl.

'So,' said Franco, deciding he'd also rather wait for the fresh pot.

'Indeed,' said the first man, smiling.

The second man said nothing, instead checking that there really was no Victoria sponge left.

'This is jolly,' said the first man. 'Oh, my turn I think. The toilets were which way?'

'That way,' pointed Franco.

The man returned a few minutes later shaking his hands.

'I must remember that casting off technique. Very clever. Thank you so much for showing it to me,' said the older woman, patting Grubber on the hand. 'Oh, is that the time? I must be off,' and she disappeared in a puff of pink smoke.

The two men disappeared in a similar fashion, leaving

Franco and Grubber with a pile of used cups and dirty plates.

'Evening.' A bulk monster in a boiler suit appeared out of the glaring whiteness. 'Don't worry. They'll be back in a minute. Just hold on while I fiddle with the switch.'

'They're a recording?' asked Franco.

'Well, not so much a recording, more a slip out of time. See, your old lady there.' He pointed to where the puff of smoke had been. 'Got her needles in a twist, didn't she? She forgot to carry the wool forward before starting the next row. Looped herself out of time. Now she's stuck there till she manages to pick up the thread again.'

'And the blokes?'

He sniffed. 'Not sure about them. Guess they must have dropped a stitch or something. Although, if you ask me, they were never the full row to start with, if you catch my drift. Still, who am I to question the ways of the world? Some of us were meant to graft and some of us were meant for higher things, even if we don't know our fair isle from our faux pas. Still, it's a job, innit? There we go.' He pressed something, and there was a sound like a fan starting up. 'If it stops in the middle or starts juddering, just give it a swift kick. That usually gets it going again. Right, that's me off for a tea break. Nice meeting you. Bye then.'

'Bye,' chimed the pair.

The whirring sound sped up, then stopped. And back were the two men and the older woman, along with a selection of as yet untouched sandwiches and cakes, and a hot pot of fresh tea.

'This is jolly,' said the first man. 'Tea anyone?'

'Not for me,' said the older woman. 'I'm still trying to remember where I put my knitting. Ah, there it is,' she smiled, not moving out of her chair. 'Now if I can pick up where I left off.' Her brows furrowed slightly. 'Hmm, I'm sure there's something not quite right there. Never mind, I'm sure it'll come to me. Perhaps a ham and relish sandwich first. Geoffrey, sandwiches first, cake later. It's the only way.'

Geoffrey, the second man, marked out a piece of Victoria sponge with his eyes, and took a crustless chicken and mayonnaise sandwich without smiling.

'This is jolly,' said the first man. 'Oh, my turn, I think. The toilets are which way?'

Franco pointed.

The first man returned a minute later, shaking his hands, then reached for a slice of Swiss roll.

'Do either of you knit?' asked the older woman.

Franco and Grubber both shook their heads.

'Pity. I've reached a part where I'm not sure whether I need to cast off or start another row. Never mind, I'll come back to it later. It's probably time we returned to our original discussion. Geoffrey, if you'd like to start.'

Geoffrey looked startled, as if he'd been caught scoffing the last of the Victoria sponge, which he had. He made a half strangled coughing sound, and prepared to speak.

'Wait a minute. There's definitely something not right. Maybe I dropped a stitch earlier or something. Would you hold it for me while I look for the pattern? Thank you.' And then puff, back to being pink smoke.

Once again, Franco and Grubber were the only ones sitting at the table. Except this time Franco could see, in his mind's eye, a rather chunky, uneven piece of pink knitting. 'She's not very good, is she?'

Grubber shook his head.

'What am I meant to do with it now? Should it not have disappeared along with them or something?' He tilted his head to see if he could get the knitting to move, but it wouldn't budge.

'You want it?'

Grubber shook his head again.

Franco sighed. 'Guess we'd better hit the button and see if she'll take it back.'

The stalblagger hit the button. Fresh sandwiches and cakes appeared. The two men and the older woman appeared.

'This is jolly,' said the first man, and hid the Victoria sponge under a tea cosy when the second man wasn't looking. The older woman was busy looking for her knitting.

'Is this it?' asked Franco.

The woman looked for a moment.

'Is it angora?' she asked.

'I don't know,' said Franco.

'Because if it is, it isn't mine. Oh, yes please.'

The first man poured out the tea.

'It's pink,' said Franco helpfully.

'Give it here and I'll have a look. Dear me, look at the state of that. That's never my handiwork. Here, take it back.'

Franco blocked her with a slice of Battenberg.

She frowned, then turned and smiled sweetly at the stalblagger, but he was already up and off to the toilet, shaking his hands in preparation for the return trip. 'Oh well, it looks like I'll have to unravel it and start something new. Perhaps Geoffrey, you'd care to. . .'

But Geoffrey was too busy cutting himself a slice of tea cosy.

The muscles on the woman's face battled to sit somewhere between a scowl and a frown with an overlay of smirk. She sighed theatrically, and shoved the knitting into a dark recess of her mind.

The stalblagger sat back down, and helpfully pointed out where she'd left it, then realised his mistake when she handed it over. More pink smoke ensued.

Equally unable to shift the knitting, the stalblagger changed it from pink to blue, stuck a gold star in the middle of it, added a fringe to the bottom, and left it where the older woman couldn't possibly miss it, but did.

The next time everything went up in pink smoke, Franco and Grubber hid under the table, along with the Victoria sponge. No-one came looking for them, but a lot of tutting could be heard.

Eventually Franco got out from under the table, cake in hand, turned it upside down on the table, set fire to the imaginary knitting, poured himself a cold cup of tea, and dropped a ham sandwich in it.

They all sat in silence.

'Well, this is. . .' said the first man.

'Quite,' said the older woman.

Geoffrey decided he didn't like Battenberg.

'Shall we?' asked the older woman.

'Indeed,' said the first man. Then all three of them got up and walked away.

'Well, I'll be,' said the bulk monster in the boiler suit, who had chosen that moment to come back in. 'Guess that's one less job to do,' and walked off.

'Does no-one round here know the word thank you?' said Franco. 'You'd think if I sorted the woolly loop whatsit thingy, I'd at least get a thank you.'

The Battenberg cake gave it a try, but spelling doesn't come naturally to sponge based life forms with marzipan edging, and so it gave up. But not before managing to form the letter L.

Franco ate the Battenberg.

Grubber stirred his mug of tea with the key for the toilet.

'This is nice, isn't it?'

'Indeed.'

They fell into a silent reverie.

'I hope they come along with some more hot water soon. I'm parched.'

The stalblagger took a sip of cold tea, and had to agree.

They waited.

They waited some more.

'This is. . .'

'Indeed.'

And as one they got up, went into the alcove, and returned via the way they'd come.

Chapter Fourteen

'And it's super, really. I know it makes your teeth fall out, but when there's such a choice of teeth around to replace them, it's not a problem, really. Although I must admit it does make chewing slightly difficult. But mustn't grumble. It's just as well I like jelly. It used to be a problem when I had my own teeth, but now they're somebody else's, it's not really a problem. But it'd be nice to have a burger now and then, for old time's sake. But I can't complain really. The jelly really is very nice, even if it is always raspberry.'

During their absence from the mine, Franco and Grubber somehow appeared to have made friends with a pompom creature.

'You were never a librarian, were you?' asked Franco.

'Oh goodness me, no,' said the pompom, stopping what it was doing. 'Apparently I was too noisy. I know, me! Can you believe it? But there you go,' and it gave a replacement teeth grin, before returning to what it was doing.

Franco and Grubber weren't entirely sure what that was, but copied the creature and hoped for the best.

'I must say, you're both very good at it. It took me years

to learn it, but you seem to have picked it up very quickly. I guess some of us are naturally gifted and some of us have to work our way from the bottom up, like a worm on a set of stairs, a very greasy set of stairs, with escalators going up either side to remind us how lowly and worm-like we really are, and even then they still have to rub it in by. . .' It gave a little cough and smiled. 'All in the past now, all forgotten. Raspberry jelly, I like raspberry jelly. Do you like raspberry jelly? I do. Especially after a hard day's work.'

'Broogle brain,' whispered Grubber to Franco.

'What?'

'Broogle brain. It has been in the mine too long. It has affected its brain.'

'I thought it just affected your teeth.'

'That is how it reaches the brain, through the teeth.'

Franco resisted the urge to put a protective hand round his molars.

The pompom looked at them quizzically. 'What was that? What do you know? What aren't you telling me? Officer, Officer, there are two interlopers here, two spies in our midst. Officer.'

'What is it?' A bulk monster loomed over them.

The pompom gave an ill-fitting smile and pointed at Franco and Grubber. 'Interlopers, Officer. Spies. They know something we don't and they won't say what it is.'

The bulk monster looked the pompom up and down, opened the hatch to a chute in the wall, and threw the pompom in. The last sound they heard it make was 'Wheeeeeeeeee!'

The bulk monster shut the hatch. 'Back to work,' he said, and walked away.

Franco shuffled a few bits of broogle, then shuffled them again. 'Any idea where that chute goes?'

The stalblagger looked thoughtful, pausing from his work. 'Down?'

'That's what I thought,' said Franco. 'Any idea what kind of Down?'

The stalblagger decided to grade the broogle by colour, but still wasn't sure. He shook his head.

'Me neither,' said Franco. 'Only, we've already tried Up, and that wasn't much use, and I doubt we could find our way back to the gift shop, even if we wanted to, and I'm thinking, well, what's the harm? I mean, if we're going to get chucked in the chute anyway, why not go now? I'd much rather do it now than wait till my brain starts falling out. What do you think?'

Grubber looked at the hatch and wondered how much breathing in would be required. Then he gave a nod.

'Actually, this isn't half bad,' said Franco, 'for a chute.'

The stalblagger would have answered, if he hadn't been busy counting the seconds till he could breathe out again. The only thing was, each time he breathed out, he got stuck in the chute, so progress was slow. And he was also beginning to get fed up with Franco sitting on his head, something that also happened on every out breath.

'It's a very smooth surface. Wonder what it's made of.'

3, 4, 5, 6.

Franco gave it a tap.

7, 8, 9, 10.

'D'you have any ideas?'

And breathe out.

'Hey, careful! You didn't tell me you were going to stop there.'

And breathe in, and in again, and see if we can't get the little narkle to go past us. And breathe out.

'Hey, you did it again.'

And reach up, and strangle quietly.

'Look,' said Franco. I can see light at the bottom there. At least I think it's light, or is it your bottom? No, it's definitely light. Let's do it in a oner. I'll hold onto your hands and you breathe in. Wheeeeeeee!'

Chapter Fifteen

The pair landed with a whump on a garishly striped sun lounger. Franco got up and moved to the next sun lounger, which was more subdued in colour, but still stripy. Grubber looked at the Franco-shaped dent in his tummy, then, holding his nose and taking a sharp breath in, popped it out again.

They surveyed the scene. They appeared to be at some kind of beach-themed cocktail bar, complete with inflatable plastic palms, beachcomber style drinks bar, and a paddling pool filled with sand. There was even a spotlight masquerading as a sun, and a background recording of waves crashing on the shore.

'Well, this is almost, I was going to say pleasant, but I swear that sun's already giving me a heat rash.' Franco got up, took off his socks, danced about in the sand, and put his socks back on, making sure not to completely manage to get all the sand off his feet first, so as to have something to complain about later. He sat back down and perused the cocktail menu. '"*Double Brainer*,"' he read out loud. '"Pineapple, banana and mango puree with a double shot of broogle juice. Guaranteed

to hit both hemispheres at once. *No Brainer.* Pure fruit juice."
Ha, ha, ha, very good. What's this one here? "*Numb Skull.*
Broogle juice with a dash of rum and half a pineapple. Like
a woolly jumper in your brain." Bit strange that one. "*Brain
Dead.* Liquorice-infused broogle juice with aniseed and
cayenne pepper. For the hangover from hell." That's the one
for me, eh? What are you having?'

The stalblagger would have answered, but for the little
creature flying out of the chute and landing with a whump
on top of him. But before it could find a sun lounger of its
own, the creature, which turned out to be an underwashed
scurzel in an 'Am I Wacky or What?' t-shirt, was dragged
off by a couple of bulk monsters who appeared not to notice
Franco and Grubber at all.

Grubber looked at the scurzel shaped dent in his tummy
and sighed, which was the best option in the circumstances,
as another creature was now on a flight path towards him.
Two more bulk monsters – or was it the same two? –
appeared to take it away.

'Em, excuse me,' called Franco.

The monsters stopped. 'The barman'll be along in a
minute,' said the nearest one.

'No, not that. Well, actually, yes, I could murder a Brain
Dead. No, what I was wondering was where you're taking
them.'

'To get their brains drained. Enjoy your drinks.'

'What do you mean to get their. . . Oh, they're gone. I
wanted to ask them a bit more. Never mind.' He returned
to the cocktail menu. "'*Brain Wash.* Broogle juice, champagne

and vanilla ice-cream. Like putting your brain on spin cycle. The vanilla ice-cream can be omitted for those who like to wash at a higher temperature. Ask your barman for more details."' Franco looked up. 'All this talk of brains isn't half off-putting. I mean, naming all your cocktails after brain themed stuff is pretty weird, and then taking all those creatures away to drain their. . . Oh, oh boy, you don't think. . . Do you? Oh boy. Suddenly I don't feel very thirsty. In fact, I think I'm going to be sick. Are you listening? Stop holding your nose. It's not like I've farted or anything.'

The stalblagger's tummy popped out.

'Are you really trying to make me sick or what? All those creatures are getting dragged off and turned into cocktails, and all you can do is lie there sticking your tummy out like some overgrown peach. I say we've got to do something. I say we've got to rescue those creatures and get their brains back out of the drinks cabinet. I say we rise up and fight back against those who would keep us down, the forces that steal our brains and turn us into mere receptacles for diced pineapple and jungle-themed swizzle sticks. Say no to the tyranny of broogle juice. Stand up on your sun lounger and say loud and proud there's nothing wrong with being stripy, unless of course you prefer dots. You can keep your plastic palm trees. I, for one, will not be swayed by the lure of the paper parasol. I am a banana and no-one can ever take that away from me. Oh, where are you taking me? What's going on? You can't drinkeralise me. You can't.' Franco struggled as two – the same two? – bulk monsters picked him up under the oxters, carried him across the room, and stuck him in a cupboard.

'Thank God for that,' said one monster. 'He was doing my head in. Are you sure he's not mad?'

'No, too many of his own teeth,' said the other. 'Takes a trained eye to spot the difference. Now come on, there's a new batch due any minute.'

It was really dark and cramped in the cupboard.

'It's really dark and cramped in here,' said Franco. 'And that's before you came in.'

The stalblagger tried to adjust his position, but only succeeded in banging his elbow off the brass display rail.

They stayed in that position for a few more minutes.

'This is stupid,' said Franco. The stalblagger had to agree. And so they both opened the door of the cupboard and got out.

Chapter Sixteen

'So, rescue mission time. Any ideas?'

Grubber shook his head and drew a blank, then chucked it in the basket before anyone could trip over it.

'Do we have to wear special costumes or anything? Only, I've never done anything like this before.'

Grubber didn't think so.

'So, it's a case of going in and taking it from there, I guess. What happens if we get captured?'

'We have too many teeth,' said Grubber.

'I never thought my safety would depend on still having a strongly attached back molar,' said Franco. 'Oh well, here goes nothing. Ready?'

Grubber nodded.

Once they'd asked directions to the Brain Drain room, it was pretty easy to find.

They opened the door, and walked into a very pleasant reception area, with squashy sofas, low beech coffee tables and real plants.

'Can I help you?' asked the receptionist.

'We're here on a mission,' said Franco.

'Do you have an appointment?'

'Didn't you hear us? We're here on a mission.'

The receptionist's face showed she was well used to dealing with heroic types, and this time would be no different. 'I'm afraid I can't help you without an appointment.'

'Yes but. . .'

'Maybe you should try Mission Accomplished down the hall. They should be able to help.'

'But it's here we want.'

The receptionist appeared unmoved by this declaration.

'We're on a really important mission.'

Silence.

'What do you have to do to get an appointment round here?'

More silence.

'Actually, how do you make an appointment? Can we make one?'

'Of course. When would you like to make one for?'

'When do you have one available?'

'10:40.'

The large clock on the wall read 10:42.

'Um, hasn't that already passed?'

'It's our next available appointment.'

'God, all this rescue mission stuff isn't all it's cracked up to be. I wonder how far Roadrail Betty would have got if he'd had to wait for an appointment. "I'm sorry sir, you can't start the rescue for half an hour." "But they'll all have

137

drowned by then." "Sorry sir, but your appointment isn't for half an hour." Kind of takes the surprise out of it.'

'We find it works for us,' said the receptionist.

'Okay, we'll take it,' said Franco, and half disappeared into a squashy sofa.

Grubber had half disappeared into another one.

'Okay, you can go in now,' said the receptionist.

'What?' Franco looked up at the clock. It said 10:40.

'Down the corridor and it's the first on the left. You can't miss it.'

They appeared to be part of a queue.

'So much for their appointment system,' muttered Franco to Grubber.

'Welcome everyone.' A smile in a blue buttoned suit and name badge appeared in front of the group. 'And welcome to our guided tour of the Brain Drain Facility, where we produce our award winning broogle drink. Will those of you who are not actually interested in the tour, but are only taking part in order to receive the free taster at the end, please proceed to the drinks kiosk where you will find a wide array of drinks and nibbles at exorbitant prices. Thank you.'

Franco and Grubber appeared to be the only ones left.

The smile continued. 'Our drink was first invented a long, long time ago when. . .'

'Excuse me, we're here on a rescue mission,' said Franco.

The smile frowned at the interruption. 'When our, oh, what's the point? Down that metal staircase there.'

138

'Thanks.'

'Don't mention it.'

'Tea break? What d'you mean they're on a tea break?' Franco was dumbfounded.

The creature in the white boiler suit who'd broken this unexpected news just shrugged its shoulders and walked off.

'Tea break. They're all on a bloody tea break.' Franco turned to Grubber and told him the news, even though he was standing right next to him. 'I mean, how inconsiderate is that? How are we supposed to rescue anyone if they're all on tea break? You know, I've got a good mind to put in a formal complaint. You can't go round doing that to people, going on a break whenever you feel like it. You don't know who's about to appear and carry out a rescue. I mean, how are we meant to do that if there's no-one around, answer me that? Exactly. You can't. And neither can I. Which means only one thing. . . Eh, what does it mean? I'm not sure, but I'll tell you something for nothing, I'm still going to put in a superhero expenses form. They can't blame me if there was no-one around to rescue. Show me someone who was needing rescuing and I'd have been straight in there, no holding back.'

'You can rescue me.'

'Mind not interrupting? Like I was saying. . . Who the hell are you?' Franco found himself looking down at a tie-dyed scurzel in a t-shirt three sizes too big for it, or was it the t-shirt that was tie dyed? It was hard to say

'You can rescue me.'

'All right, I heard you the first time. How come you're not on tea break like everyone else?'

The scurzel thought about this. 'I don't like chocolate biscuits.'

'Definitely a broogle brain we've got here,' whispered Franco to Grubber.

'I heard that,' said the scurzel.

So Franco whispered quieter.

Thankfully, the stalblagger's lip reading skills weren't what they once were and it could thus disregard anything Franco might be saying.

'So.' Now that Grubber was fully up to speed, Franco decided to question the scurzel a little closer. 'So, why don't you like chocolate?'

'It gives me a rash.'

'What's your favourite colour?'

'Blue.'

'I thought you said green.'

'No, yellow.'

'Damn, this guy is good,' whispered Franco.

The stalblagger smiled and nodded.

'What's the capital of Portugal?'

'Brazil.'

'How many monkeys can you fit in a barrel?'

'Depends on the size of the monkey.'

Franco thought carefully, and spoke slowly. 'If I showed you which way was up and you knew there was a rainbow rising, hold on, I'm not finished yet, there was a rainbow

140

rising, what colour would the grass have to be painted, I'm not finished. . .'

The scurzel frowned.

'What colour would the grass have to be painted in order to stop the penguins falling asleep?' Franco folded his arms in triumph and waited for the reply.

The scurzel furrowed its brow in thought. Grubber handed it a calculator and a plastic rabbit. 'Thanks,' said the scurzel, and handed them back. Eventually it was ready to reply. 'Tulips.'

'Explain,' said Franco.

'Penguins aren't allowed either side of a rainbow without a permit, and even if they did have one, it depends on the grass being on the right side of up, thus making any colour irrelevant.'

'And the tulips?'

'A penguin's favourite flower.'

Franco looked to Grubber for confirmation.

Grubber confirmed.

'Consider yourself rescued,' said Franco, and shook the scurzel's hand.

'What next?' asked the scurzel.

'Em, I'm not exactly sure,' said Franco. Grubber handed him a scarf. 'Eh, apparently we wrap you up warmly.'

'Why's that?'

'Eh, why's that?' Franco looked at Grubber. 'Em, because the relief of being rescued often leads to a drop in body temperature.'

'Yes, I am feeling somewhat chilly.'

'Well, this should do it,' said Franco, and wrapped the scarf around the scurzel. 'Oh, and a bobble hat too. That should definitely keep the heat in.'

'How do I look?' asked the scurzel and gave a twirl.

'Like a vision in wool.'

'Really?'

'Absolutely. Now let's go and collect our Mission Accomplished certificates, and then I don't know about you, but I could fair go a cup of tea and a biscuit after that.' He saw the scurzel's worried expression. 'Don't worry, you can have a cracker.'

The scurzel smiled.

'Off we go. Or rather, we would if there wasn't a great big bulk monster standing right in front of us. Hello, how can we help you?'

'Where do you think you lot are going?'

'We're heading off for a cup of tea now you're finished. Hope you've left a few biscuits for the rest of us.'

'We only have biscuits on a Thursday. This ain't Thursday.'

'Snowballs?'

'Tuesday afternoon.'

'Garibaldis?'

'That's a biscuit.'

'Is it? I always had it down as a cake that wasn't quite sure, either that or had been trodden on and left out of the biscuit tin overnight.'

'That makes it a biscuit.'

'Does it? Oh well, I guess you're the expert. Nice chatting to you. Better get going before they run out of teabags.'

'Just hold on there. What are you lot doing here in the first place?'

'We're on a rescue mission, but since there doesn't seem to be anyone to rescue, we've decided to give up and go for a cup of tea instead; drown our sorrows in a mug of the wet stuff, so to speak.'

'No-one told me about any rescue mission.'

'Well, check it out with reception upstairs. We were definitely booked in for one.'

The bulk monster thought about believing them, and decided not to. But before he'd quite managed to reach that decision, the scurzel, who till that point had been quietly bouncing up and down, bounced up higher and smacked the bulk monster in the chin, jolting his head backwards, which wouldn't in itself have been a problem if the stalblagger hadn't been holding an anvil there for it to smack against.

They looked at the gently concussed form lying on the floor.

'I don't think anyone told him about that either,' said Franco. 'Cup of tea anyone?'

Chapter Seventeen

None of the creatures appeared to notice when a stalblagger, a human and a scurzel in a red hat and scarf clutching a Mission Accomplished Certificate entered the canteen. Maybe it was because they'd already left and gone back to work.

'Budge up there,' said Franco, sitting down next to Grubber with a tray piled high with all sorts of snacks and edibles. 'This rescue mission stuff makes you really hungry, eh? Did you know we didn't have to pay for this lot either? They've got a permanent rescue mission tab at the till there. Well, bon voyage or whatever it is they say down at the local deli. This looks like top nosh to me.'

The scurzel nibbled delicately at its plain cracker as it watched the other two tuck into piles of bacon, sausages and anything else that could be flung in a pan or on a hotplate, all washed down with copious amounts of tea. The scurzel sipped at a mineral water.

'So, now that we've rescued you, what have you got planned next?' asked Franco.

This seemed to panic the scurzel. Either that or it had

decided to practise its look of panic face at that very moment. It shuffled a paper napkin in lieu of an answer.

'Only we've got to head off now. Don't want to still be here when the next rescue mission comes rolling in. That could be a bit awkward, especially when we've already got our certificate.'

'You could come with us,' said Grubber.

At this, the little scurzel's face lit up.

Franco scowled. 'Um, well, I don't know about that. It's not like we're contractually obliged or anything. And it's already got a new hat and scarf out of it. What more could you want?'

'I like it.'

'Oh well then, be my guest. If I invited along everyone I liked we'd be. . . well, we'd be. . . that's not the point and you know it. Where's that trifle I ordered?' Franco stomped off.

And not for the first time in their epic journey, the Badge Kit saved the day.

'Well.' Franco sat back down, trifle-less, and peered at the scurzel's chest to try to read the name. He turned to the stalblagger. 'What does that say? I always struggle with Gothic script.'

'Pod,' said Grubber, and looked surprised. He turned the badge round. 'Pod,' said Grubber.

Pod smiled.

'Pod? That's not much of a name, is it? Is it short for something?'

The scurzel looked at Grubber.

'Probably,' said Grubber.

'Something too long for a badge, is it? Isn't that always the way? You'd think they'd make badges bigger or something, or at least restrict the size of names so you wouldn't get this problem. Still, what can you do? Ah great, my trifle. Thank you.' A creature put down a trifle in front of him. 'What's up?'

The stalblagger and the scurzel stared.

The trifle was the size of a big bowl.

'So I like trifle. Is that a problem? You guys can get your own, although I think this is the last banana and grapefruit.'

For no reason, other than that it felt like it, the trifle began to shrink. Franco sat with spoon poised, watching his ever dwindling dessert, until it grew so small it had technically disappeared, although it had at least had the courtesy to leave the maraschino cherry behind.

Grubber ate the cherry.

Franco hit Grubber with the spoon.

Grubber offered the cherry back.

Franco declined. 'So that's us ready to go then?' he asked, and gave Grubber a poke in the eye. Grubber gave him it back, just in case Franco needed it later.

Pod wondered if anyone would notice if he took his badge off and found his own way out of here.

'Come on, hurry up,' said Franco, grabbing three complimentary lollies on his way out. The scurzel quickly donned his hat and scarf. And Grubber made Franco put the lollies back because they wouldn't shut up once you took the wrapper off them, and even if you did manage to get them as far as your mouth, the voices rattled around in your head and spoilt any flavour sensation you might be enjoying, even if that was strawberry and vanilla. Not that it mattered, as the bus they were about to get on would drown out even the loudest lolly.

'Good welcome and thank you for joining us today on Rubicon Tours. We hope you're all enjoying your trip with us and take home many happy mementos, remembering that any items left behind will be destroyed upon your departure. Thank you once more, and enjoy the rest of the trip.' The speaker system on the bus crackled out of life, and all was the quiet murmurings of sweetie wrappers, unfully digested burps and barely suppressed nasal cadences.

Franco tried to check if the drool from the creature asleep next to him hadn't entirely soaked through his shirt, although he suspected it would still have left a stain. He discreetly shoved a paper napkin in between them and hoped this would somewhat ameliorate the damage. It hadn't been his choice to get on the tour bus waiting outside the canteen, but since it was the only bus that was waiting, they'd got on it.

Grubber was playing ping pong with the seat in front of him, and the seat was winning, while Pod suspected that Franco had left a couple of the rules out of Solitary Hide and Seek, and got out of the locker, landing with a plop next to Grubber, causing the seat to lose concentration and Grubber to score an unexpected point. By way of thank you, Grubber handed Pod a jellied fruit.

They both stared glassy-eyed through the moving window, in the way of those who have accepted the privations of too much time sitting in a cramped position with only a congested toilet for relief as somehow being a metaphor for life, if only they could get that cramp out of their left leg.

As if in sympathy with their predicament, the speaker crackled into life again and began singing in a light jazz muzak style with the merest hint of vibrato.

Franco jerked his head awake, and noticed with some satisfaction that he had in turn drooled on the creature, but unfortunately the earlier consumption of blackcurrant juice hadn't produced the desired effect.

And all too soon – or was it years later? – they all found themselves stumbling and stretching out of the bus and into a brightly lit, semi-darkened bus depot in the middle of the night.

There was a small explosion when the bus driver discovered a forgotten porcelain teacup with matching saucer at the back of the bus, followed by a scream of realisation as the owner came rushing back from wherever it was they had been, then all was still.

Apart from one little old lady. One very grim faced little old lady. And her equally grim faced little dog. 'Where is it then?' she said.

Franco could have sworn he hadn't seen her on the bus, but then again he hadn't looked too closely at where he had acquired the blackcurrant juice from either. 'Um, I thought somebody had left it as a present, like, eh, like a welcome to your seat kind of thing, only it wasn't exactly near my seat, more kind of. . .'

'What are you wittering on about?' she snapped. 'I'm not freezing my tits off for this. Give me the packlarge and we can all write merry messages to each other in Christmas cards or whatever it is you folk do in your part of the world.'

The little dog growled, just to let them know it wouldn't be sending them a Christmas card anytime soon either.

'Um.'

'Okay, name your price. Your type always have a price. I told them I wouldn't pay anything, but I expect they'll try to pass it off as an import tax or something.'

'Packlarge?'

'Is one satsuma enough? It's your own fault I don't have any oranges, as I've already explained to the guy on the phone. Take it, and I hope you choke on it.' She held it out.

Franco wasn't sure he could grab it quicker than the dog could grab him.

The old woman stuck the satsuma back in her pocket and squinted at him. 'I can't work out whether you're being deliberately obtuse or naturally imbecilic. Whichever way, I think I'm better dealing with the creature next to you. My packlarge.'

Grubber handed over the *Pearls of Nebulus* book.

'I hope you washed your hands first.'

Grubber looked at his hands and was pleased to see that he hadn't.

She flicked through it. 'It all seems to be there. But if I

find out any of it's missing, I'll be straight on the phone. Now go away.' And off she went.

The little dog gave them one last snarl, then trotted after her.

'A satsuma? What's that all about? We trek halfway across the universe with that bloody book, not to mention the up and down bits, and all she offers us is one bloody satsuma. And we didn't even get to keep it. It's like Santa Claus wrapping up a present in a mousetrap and then accusing you of stealing the biscuits. Hey, where are you two going? Aren't you even the tiniest bit bothered? What's this?'

Grubber handed him a bus ticket, and a satsuma.

'Ha, ha, ha. Did you take it when the old biddy wasn't looking? Bet you it's bitter.'

Then Grubber handed Franco the original book. It glowed softly in his hand. Grubber opened it, chucked in the satsuma, and shut it again. There was a brief citrusy glow.

'Hey, how come the book gets to eat it? I only said I thought it might be bitter. I didn't mean you to chuck it. Well, I hope you enjoyed it.' This he said to the book.

The book said nothing.

'And how come we've got the book anyway? I just saw Mrs Snarky walk off with it.'

Grubber gave the nearby bookstand a light turn, indicating a gap in the display, and smiled.

'Oh, brilliant. But I wouldn't like to be you when she finds out she's been diddled.'

Grubber handed him another book, this time from the stand. *The Pearls of Nebulus* said the cover. And right enough,

150

if you ignored the three for two sticker, the different type-face and jacket cover, and the fact that it was a paperback rather than a hardback, you could, assuming you were standing in a randomly lit bus depot at night, easily mistake one for the other, especially if you'd forgotten your reading glasses and couldn't remember what the original looked like in the first place.

'My arm's killing me,' complained Franco, putting both the copy and the original back on the stand.

Pod began frantically banging on the bus window and waving through the glass at them from his specially selected seat with booster cushion.

The bus engine rumbled. Franco suddenly realised what the bus ticket was for. 'Right enough, I haven't even begun to test the full range of drool and fruit juice combinations. Hey Pod, Pod, ever played Pin the Blind Donkey?' he yelled and leapt on board.

Grubber glanced at the bookstand, but didn't see anything he hadn't read before. He climbed up the steps of the bus, and the doors whooshed closed behind him.

The bus eased its way out of the depot and headed off into the night. All fell silent and still, save for the sound of a satsuma being spat out.

'Too bitter.'

The Five & Three Song

Kerri Anderson

What do you do when you've got five a - li - ens?

What do you do when you've got just three

What do you do when you've got five a - li - ens?

Stick them down the mines and then have a cup of tea.

'What do you do when you've got five laser beams?
What do you do when you've got just three?
What do you do when you've got five laser beams?
Cut up a banana and then sit it on your knee.

'What do you do when you've got five spacerships?
What do you do when you've got just three?
What do you do when you've got five spacerships?
Grab another ten and take o'er the galaxy.'

152